# FIREFLIES

*A Celtic Romance Series*

## Shea Hulse

ISBN-13: 978-1-7378471-0-6

Cover design by: Fiverr
Library of Congress Control Number: 2018675309
Printed in the United States of America

*To my family.*

# CONTENTS

Title Page

Copyright

Dedication

Prologue                                                    4

Chapter 1                                                   5

Chapter 2                                                  17

Chapter 3                                                  25

Chapter 4                                                  34

Chapter 5                                                  47

Chapter 6                                                  64

Chapter 7                                                  74

Chapter 8                                                  96

Chapter 9                                                 111

Chapter 10                                               148

Chapter 11                                               177

Chapter 12                                               193

Chapter 13                                               207

Acknowledgement                                          216

About The Author                                         218

Books In This Series                                     220

*A Celtic Romance Series*

**SHEA HULSE**

*In my frenzy, I ran into something without realizing it. Big hands closed over my shoulders as I gripped the chest they belonged to. Under other circumstances, I'd be elated. Green eyes stared back at me, his reddish hair hidden beneath a baseball cap, huge frame swallowing mine easily.*

Bridget had never considered herself special, odd sure, but nothing worth looking at twice. And she had never cared to be looked at twice, either.

**Until Declan, that is.**

Then one night Bridget is approached by a strange (and large) dog. Rescued by Declan, he reveals that Bridget may be special after all. And the dog has been sent to protect her.

Does she have the strength to defeat a powerful witch and her three sons? Why is Declan involved in magic and mystery, anyway? And can she save Ruad, her handsome mentor in this new world? As they dig deeper, they uncover that they all have more in common than just their troubled pasts.

*The Ulster Cycles are a part of Irish mythology, and this novel depicts characters from the old stories in a new and creative light. While much is taken from these oral stories, this novel is a historical romance loosely based on them.* **With magic, mystery, and romance involved, this is a novel about discovering your hidden potential and celebrating your authentic self.**

# PROLOGUE

In general, I liked being a wallflower. All throughout school I floated from group to group, never belonging to anyone in particular but welcome in most.

I did the same at home.

Sometimes it was lonely. But occasionally people floated in to keep me company for a while.

Like Declan. He's been around for a while, and he makes me feel less lonely. And a little more understood.

It took a lot of time (and too much alcohol) before I understood more. The loneliness was only part of it.

Beneath all the pain of not belonging was the realization that I didn't want to belong. Not to (most of) my family and not to most of the groups I hung around.

They weren't my cup of tea.

My experience was that people were untrustworthy and cruel. Or I was just trying to fit in with cruel and untrustworthy people, either or.

I just wanted to be normal. And accepted.

Now I know that some of the worst people hide behind normal. They wear it like an invisibility cloak, covering all of their ugliness with fake smiles.

And acceptance is overrated.

So I melted into the background, hoping they wouldn't single me out. Because no one likes things they can't understand.

If only I knew then just how different I really was.

# CHAPTER 1

"For fuck's sake," I mumbled under my breath as I was making my way out of work.

Not that I didn't ocassionally enjoy my job, but some days were better than others. More than anything, it was the meaningless manner of my job that irked me. Providing excellent customer service at a restaurant filled my bank account, but it didn't cure my existential dread.

There certainly had to be more to life than this. But what? Cursing seemed to ease the emptiness, so I did it fairly often.

While I ambled down the parking lot toward my car, feeling an ache in every bone and muscle in my body, I added it all up.

Forty-nine hours this week—not bad. Little time for much else given my hours were the opposite of most typical jobs.

Not that there was much else. No boyfriend, few friends, plenty of family I could do without. Sure, I loved them, but they were better in small doses.

I liked to keep to myself, anyway. It's simpler.

Books were my main friends. They comforted me, kept me company, and never let me down.

Books and Declan.

It was already past midnight, so that was the plan. Go home, lose myself in a book and see if sleep won't drag me under. I really was hoping it would.

I tend to get myself in trouble when it doesn't.

Almost to my car, I saw the same dog as always. A great big Irish wolfhound, so out of place in the middle of the suburbs of New Jersey.

But he was always there in his spot near the mechanic. I assumed the mechanic was his owner.

I also assumed it was a he, though I'd never been close enough to him to know for sure. Don't care to get close enough either.

But he was always outside, and he always stuck to his garage, watching me.

He was always watching me.

Maybe it's not that exciting in the garage, or not that comfortable.

Regardless of the reason, there he was with his dark wiry hair and big frame, his head leaning on his paws and cool gaze assessing me. It was unnerving.

I love dogs, and they don't bother me normally. But there was something about his gaze that irked me. He stared right through me with an intelligent gaze that didn't seem to belong to a dog.

Then there was his size. I'm not big. At five foot nothing and one hundred twenty pounds. I might have a muscular frame, but the dog was huge.

All wiry, pitch-black fur, he must have outweighed me by thirty pounds at least and was probably as tall as my shoulder. I didn't need to get close enough to test that.

If a dog can lick my face without any effort, I get a little leery. One snap taking my face off comes to mind.

It was a cold night though, so I hurried on, snuggling closer into my jacket to fight off the wind. Hoping my fast pace wouldn't bring more attention to me and invoke the massive dog to chase after me.

As if by thinking it, I caught the dog's attention. His ears perked up and twitched some. Then the big dog lumbered to his feet.

Damn it.

My brain started seizing up. I knew I wasn't supposed to run because that would only make him want to chase me. And yet, I was so close to my car if I just scurried quickly I should make it there before him.

I opted for the latter and with one heave I was off, not quite running but definitely not walking. Hoping beyond hope that the dog wasn't about to chase me.

A quick glance told me I was wrong.

His giant frame was definitely headed my way. And with his long legs he was eating up ground fast.

My hopes of making it to the car were dwindling, and I set my sights on jumping on top of something. The only problem being that anything I could climb up, the dog probably could too.

In my frenzy, I ran into something solid. Big hands closed over my shoulders as I gripped the chest they belonged to. My heart was in my throat and the adrenaline spiked like never before.

"Declan!" I exclaimed, realizing it was my coworker's arms I'd found myself in. Under other circumstances, I'd be elated. Green eyes stared back at me, his reddish hair hidden beneath a baseball cap, huge frame swallowing mine easily.

"Bridget! It's ok, breathe. He won't hurt you," he said back, his slight brogue more prominent in his urgency.

With panic still gripping me firmly, I swiveled my head to find the behemoth of a dog.

Sitting on his heels, the big dog stared back at me, level with my gaze. I didn't want to challenge him, so I quickly looked down. More like so he didn't bite my face off.

Taking a second to quickly inhale Declan's scent, I savored his warmth as I relaxed a little in his hold. Broad shoulders and barrel chest surrounded me, with one giant hand on my neck holding me closer.

I'd really like to run my hands along his back for a minute, but I thought that would be inappropriate. Well, I knew it was, but I wanted to anyway.

Normally I only looked at Declan as my friend. Keeping him at arm's length meant I could keep him; it was uncomplicated. This was not arm's length. Now my heart was beating wildly for a completely different reason.

As I regretfully extricated myself from his embrace, I mumbled stupidly, "Thanks." For lack of something better to say.

Because in another part of my mind I was wondering how he knew that the dog wouldn't hurt me. And where did he come from, anyway? He'd left before me tonight. Why was he still here?

We hung out regularly, but usually, he'd wait for me if we made plans.

"Is he your dog?" I asked.

"Um, no," he responded.

"Ok...?" I prompted for further information.

He had the oddest expression on his face. And though I'd removed myself from his embrace, he still kept both hands firmly on my shoulders as he looked down at me.

His green eyes, usually filled with mirth, were cold and distant. Usually he was smiling and joking, with just the hint of ferocity that reminded you he wasn't to be messed with.

There was no mischief right now. Right now he looked deadly.

I couldn't help thinking his handsome features were significantly more attractive in their intensity. His strong jaw was set in a firm line, full lips hiding perfect white teeth, long reddish eyelashes surrounding those green eyes that were usually filled with warmth. And the freckles, those damn freckles.

"There's a lot to explain, but not here. Let's get in your car," he finally responded.

His voice brooked no argument, so I dumbly walked over to my car and unlocked it, the dog following slowly behind us. Tail low, ears up, and eyes surveying the area. He sniffed like a dog on a hunt, his hot breath tickling the back of my neck occasionally.

Declan opened the back door of my car to let the dog in.

"I thought you said he wasn't your dog?" I said, even though I didn't argue allowing the dog to accompany us. He seemed to want to.

"He's not. He's your dog, I think. Listen, it's complicated. Just get in the car. Quickly please," Declan said in a rush.

He held the door open for me and ushered me inside. His huge frame formed a barricade with the open door, shielding me from the outside.

Once he shut my door, he jogged around to the other side and threw himself in, locking the doors while he did so. It was something I did when I got freaked out in the dark by myself. When I did it, I laughed at myself, but Declan doing it had me on edge.

As he buckled himself in he said, "Drive."

"Where?" I said as I put the truck in gear, once again grateful for the larger SUV with four-wheel drive. I'm not certain Declan or the dog would have fit otherwise.

"Get on 287 North. I'll tell you what to do," he said shortly.

Ordinarily I would have argued, but I did as I was told. I wasn't a fan of being told what to do. Not accustomed to meekly obeying, I was marveling at the argument that didn't surface instead of focusing on the task at hand.

One strong hand rested on my thigh. His warmth seeped through, searing me to my core.

"Bridget, it's ok," Declan reassured me before removing his hand too soon.

White knuckles stared back at me from the steering wheel as I took a deep breath. The giant dog could be seen in my rear- view mirror. He was staring out the window, ever calm and cool. I'd traveled 287 North my entire life, so I didn't worry about where I was going, but I was curious about where we were going.

We were silent as I drove, too tense for conversation.

I'd known Declan a little while. One morning at work he'd walked up to me and introduced himself as the new waiter. Not a strange occurrence—the restaurant industry is teeming with new faces.

When he'd approached me, my brain immediately started sounding the alarm. Trouble, he was definitely trouble.

Over six foot tall, all broad shoulders, square jaw, and thick muscles, he commanded authority. Looking like he could chop down a tree and throw it over his shoulder, there weren't many to rival him in size.

Combined with the reddish hair, green eyes, and freckles, he didn't blend in with the crowd. The accent didn't hurt either.

Honestly, the only reason we weren't together was probably that he wasn't into me. Or at least that's what I told myself.

Wondering why he was waiting tables and not at least a personal trainer, I thanked my lucky stars he was waiting tables at my restaurant. We became fast friends.

Pretty quickly we learned we were the yin to the others yang. If I couldn't reach something off a shelf, he was there to get it for me. Or when the bus bucket needed emptying and it weighed a ton, he was there. When my temper got the best of me, he gave pretty good hugs. Ok really good hugs.

And when he couldn't polish a glass because his hands were too big, my tiny ones were perfect. The time he dropped a check presenter between the stand and the wall, but his arms were too big, there I was. Or when a table was super chatty, I was to charm them while he stood to the side stoically.

Though, to be fair, it was usually him rescuing me. His six foot something to my five foot nothing. My brown hair and brown eyes to his red hair and green eyes. Total opposites, but it worked.

I couldn't tell why I trusted him, but I did. Maybe it was just wishful thinking, but his presence had that effect on me. If he was around, things would be alright. That's why he was trouble. I liked having him near me too much.

"Take this exit," he said softly.

Pulled out of my reverie, I chanced a glance at his face. His jaw was tense, and he kept canvassing the area like the dog. After a few more directions and twenty more minutes, he had me turn right onto a back country road.

Yes, we have those in New Jersey.

As I turned right, he pointed to a house illuminated by floodlights. It was a huge cabin style house, large wrap-around porch, and a giant swath of green grass hidden behind trees and a wrought-iron fence. He pulled his phone out and pressed a few buttons, and the portion of the gate enclosing the driveway began opening.

"Pull in there and straight into the garage," he said.

"Okay," I mumbled back.

I trusted him, but the idea of being in his house suddenly felt too intimate. While we regularly hung out, it was usually at a diner or at my apartment. At least at my apartment, I was in control. I felt very out of control right now.

We'd gone the half hour from suburbia New Jersey to the wooded mountainous New Jersey. Not unfamiliar to me, I knew the woods. But it felt too dark tonight.

Panic began to rise again, and I felt as if I'd been punched in the gut. What was going on right now?

Before I could voice that question, warmth enveloped my neck as the giant dog started sniffing me. He gave me a big wet lick and went back to his original position.

A small smile formed on my face. I guess it was alright, if the dog was trying to settle my nerves for me. They always seem to know, don't they?

Once in the garage, I put the car in park. Declan leaned over and turned the car off. My heart sped up again as his knuckles brushed my knee.

"Listen..." he said. And then didn't say anything else.

"Listening..." I said.

He blew out a gust of air and took off his hat, running his fingers through his hair before returning the hat to his head. His obvious distress was starting to worry me more than any of the other oddities of the night.

"Do you trust me?" he asked.

What a loaded question that was.

"I mean, yeah? I'm pretty sure," I responded.

He smiled a little, and the mischief was there in his eyes. My stomach did a somersault. I was in so much trouble.

"I'll take it. Listen, we're going to go inside. I have to talk to you about something. I just want to be sure you're comfortable with that," he said.

"Now you ask me? Do I have a choice?" I responded. He'd been so demanding. Why ask for permission now?

"No. Well, of course, but no. But I'd like to hear you're okay with it. Does that make sense?"

"No. But I appreciate the sentiment, I think," I said with a hint of sarcasm.

He reached over and squeezed my hand, and my stomach did more somersaults. We touched all the time, but for some reason it felt different right now. And not just because we were about to go into his house.

This was a side I'd never seen of him before. Gone was the carefree smile, and in its place was a concerned scowl. He radiated urgency, despite his pausing to kind of ask permission.

The air was crackling with electricity.

The garage was attached to the house, and he walked ahead of me to open the door, the dog hot on his heels. The dog waited for me to go ahead though, and I was sandwiched between them as we made our way into a kitchen to rival any I'd seen in my life.

Wait, why was Declan serving tables if he lived here? He does live here, right?

"You do live here, right? This isn't like the dog thing again," I said immediately after thinking it.

"Yes, I live here."

"Then why are you waiting tables?" I questioned again.

"For you."

My mouth had gone completely dry at that. While I waited for my brain to reboot, I tried to think of a rational explanation for everything.

I failed.

He was staring at me with an intense expression, and I started to squirm under his scrutiny. The corners of his mouth tipped up and his eyes crinkled.

"You're cute when you're nervous," he said as he took a step closer.

I didn't mean to, but I took a small step back.

"Relax," he said.

Then he leaned over and kissed my cheek. Damn it but I was blushing now. Stupid Irish skin, always showing everything.

It wasn't that he'd never kissed my cheek before. We did when we said hello and goodbye. But something was different now, and we both knew it. And part of it had to do with being in his house.

The dog growled, glaring at Declan.

"I'm getting to it," he spat back.

Great, now he was talking to not-his dog.

"Come, let's sit. Are you hungry? Thirsty? Never mind. I know what you'd like. Come on and sit and I'll get you something."

"You don't have to worry about me. I'm fine," I said.

"It's the least I could do. Now come on."

He led us through the large kitchen with gray marble countertops, black shiny appliances, a huge kitchen island and breakfast bar. Above the stove was a hood like the industrial kitchens have. Plenty of dark wooden cabinets and light pinewood floors. I wondered if he had a huge family; it was too much for one person.

Oh man, what if he was married? But that wasn't likely if I'm being honest. We spent an abnormally large amount of time together. If he was married, I would have sniffed it out by now.

After the kitchen we went through an equally large dining room with the same color scheme. Long ash gray table, black railing backed chairs, and a centerpiece of sunflowers contrasted the furnishings. As I looked around the room, there were sunflower accents strewn about, a picture of a single sunflower, light yellow accents in the wainscoting.

It was like it was made for me, which wasn't comforting at the current moment.

We veered left to the living room, which was styled more as a cabin. A tall cathedral ceiling was unexpected, with the right wall made of glass, broken only by the wood logs that intersected it. Beyond the glass were woods and sky, pitch black and sinister at this hour.

To the right was a door leading to the porch overlooking a valley below. Sensing my unease, he pressed a button on the wall and automatic curtains closed off the view. It was something about the idea that anyone could be watching me, and I would have no idea that irked me about glass windows like that.

A river stone wall was directly in front of me, with a giant fireplace as the centerpiece. The hearth was cold and empty, but logs were stacked to the left. Surrounding the fireplace were overstuffed couches in an L, pointing towards the fireplace and the window, cutting the room in half.

Across from the couch was a giant TV nestled in the corner of the wall that was glass and the stone one, on a black stand. The lower half of the glass wall was closed off with logs so when you were seated you weren't on display.

It was more comfortable that way. I didn't feel like I was completely exposed. The couches were gray, with the same flooring from the kitchen and dining room. Except here, beneath the couch, was a textured gray green area rug that seemed plush and comfortable.

Again I wondered if this was Declan's decor or something else, maybe someone else. Like a wife. If he was married, it would definitely kill whatever shred of hope I had left in humanity.

The best sight of all was the wall directly opposite the glass wall. To the far left was an enclosed staircase, pine like the floors. But from the floor to the balcony and balcony to ceiling were shelves lined with books.

It ran the length of the wall until the hallway at the far right that must lead to the front door. I wanted to touch all of them.

There were even different chairs situated comfortably near the books, like we were in a coffee shop. A recliner, a rocking chair, and a love seat. All situated around a coffee table. One on the first floor and one set up on the balcony.

Oh man, there was even a window seat on the second floor. With a cushion on top and a curtain partially enclosing it. It was everything I had never allowed myself to dream about, and then some.

"Are those all yours?" I said a little breathlessly.

"Yes, I haven't read all of them yet, but I have a mind to. Go check them out while I get everything ready," he said.

Not needing further encouragement, I wandered over, running my hands gently over the spines as I read the titles. There were the classics, and modern titles, and everything in between. My hands itched to grab a few armfuls and carry them back over to the couch and remain there until the end of time. Or until I needed more books.

As I studied them, I noticed a few were quite old. Clearly vellum, well-worn, and some close to falling apart. Those I touched every gently. Feeling more at peace than I had in a lifetime, I started at Declan's touch.

"Sorry to frighten you more, but I was afraid you'd stay here forever if I let you. I brought you a change of clothes if you'd like to get more comfortable. The bathroom was back between the kitchen and dining room. If you wanted, if not it's all right," he said timidly.

This was getting curiouser and curiouser.

My stomach kept going on flipping and flopping when he looked at me like that. His hand rested on my shoulder lightly, but it was like I was on fire.

I glanced at my outfit. Underneath my coat, my black work pants and black button down smelled like the kitchen and looked like table fifty-three's mussels, sixty's crème brûlée, and everything else in between. I just wish I didn't have to stink so bad, but I worked a double today.

"I would like to change, actually. Thanks," I said with a smile.

He helped me out of my coat and took my purse for me before handing me a stack of clothes, neatly folded. I helped myself to the bathroom.

The walls were a light gray, and the towels gray with green and yellow accents. There was a shower and a tub, covered by a plain gray shower curtain, light beige tile floor, and a huge mirror hanging over the sink.

This house probably had a few more full baths tucked away in other places. I could get used to this. Unless his wife was already.

I stopped short for a second. What was I doing? What was going on right now? Was Declan expecting me to stay the night?

If so, what else was he expecting? Obviously I was attracted to him but to this point we'd only been friends and I liked it that way.

Getting romantically involved always screwed things up. Especially if there were more than two people in the equation.

I shook my head to stop my spiral. I was really confident Declan was not married, but I just don't know what was going on right now.

Every night after work, we'd do something together. We'd usually go get something to eat, and we'd sit and talk for hours. Neither of us were oblivious to what simmered beneath our friendship. It was just that I didn't think either of us wanted to ruin a good thing by getting involved.

As I pulled on his clothes, I wasn't certain that the unspoken agreement was still intact.

# CHAPTER 2

"God, what the hell is wrong with me?" I said under my breath. *A lot*, I answered in my head.

I was freshly clothed, swimming in his sweatpants and t-shirt. Looking at myself in the mirror, I wished I had something to really freshen up with. Exhausted from the busy day, I didn't look or smell my best.

But I was really enjoying wearing his clothes. Like a lot. And they smelled phenomenal.

The pang of panic hit me again. What was going on? If Declan did turn out to be a nut job I really painted myself into a corner. Or married, ugh. Why hadn't I questioned him more?

*Because you don't care; you like being near him. Nut job, married, or not*, my subconscious answered.

Truthfully, he was a balm for this inner voice I couldn't keep quiet. It kept me coming back like a drug, amongst other things...

But If he was a psycho, I imagine I would have sniffed it out by now. I spend nearly every day with him. Twelve hours a day at work and then a few hours after. There's no way he could be married either, right?

*But what about this electricity? And the kiss on the cheek?* My body went temporarily numb before the adrenaline pumped through my veins again. After a few moments of hyperventilating, I steeled myself. Only one way to find out.

*And the dog, the house, and everything in between?* my subconscious threw out there when I had my hand on the doorknob.

Because to be honest, my brain was focused significantly

more on the kiss and being in his house in his clothes right now. I couldn't care less about the rest. Well, okay, I cared a little about the rest.

Exiting the bathroom, the smell of a fire burning immediately hit me. It smelled wonderful, and I was excited about the prospect of sitting in the living room snuggled up with Declan in front of a roaring fire. With a book in my hand, kissing him...

*Ugh! Stop!* I mentally chided myself. He said he had to talk to me, and he seemed super tense about it. And besides, don't go making more out of this than it is. We're friends and we like it that way. Do not go making a fool of yourself by trying to kiss him or something.

The thought of kissing him didn't help the situation, so I shook my head to clear my thoughts a little. I needed to douse myself in ice water. My body was like a live wire, and I couldn't seem to cut the surge off.

"Are you lost?" his deep voice came from the kitchen.

*Shit.* I turned to see him smiling mischievously again, and I gave him an answering glare. His smile grew.

*Great, now he's caught me thinking inappropriate thoughts about him.*

"Come help me carry this into the other room. Are you comfortable now?" he asked.

*No*, I thought.

"Yes, thank you. Now can you please tell me what's going on?" I said with a bit of a sneer. Damn him for being so appealing.

"Yes, boss, I'll get to it. Let's just get settled in the living room."

I gave him a questioning look, and he just winked at me. Heart be still. Behave normally. Don't give yourself away. Maybe he doesn't even feel this electricity. Just put one foot in front of the other, don't trip, and go help him. And for heaven's sake, do not touch him.

When I got over to him, he gave me an assessing look. When he was finished, he leaned over and hugged me to him and kissed the top of my head. *Fuck.*

I hugged him back and melted into him a bit.

"Sorry, you look adorable," he said simply when he let me go. He went back to gathering the food he'd gotten ready for us. Taking what looked like a bowl of stew out of the microwave, he placed it next to another one on a tray and went about getting forks.

God, this was torture. What is going on? My brain was mush. I couldn't keep up. Was this all just a ploy to get me here? But why bother feeding me and clothing me if he planned on just taking them off?

*Stop!* I shouted in my head.

"What can I do?" I said instead.

"I have some herbal tea in those two mugs. Carry those in for me?" he said.

I grabbed the mugs and followed him into the living room. What a good pair of Irishmen, I mused. Hot tea, stew, and a fire. We might as well be back in Ireland. It was part of what we connected on, our shared heritage.

When he set everything down on the coffee table, I did the same. Then I suddenly panicked about where to sit. It would be stupid to sit over on the part of the couch furthest away from him if I was to eat too, but sitting too close felt...I had to bite my tongue a little to stop the thought train from gathering speed.

He solved the problem for me by sitting down first and throwing one huge arm around my waist and pulling me down to him. Settling me firmly against his side, he kept his arm around me.

I squirmed a little and with more hesitancy than I wished, I said, "Declan..."

I wanted to staunch this before it went any further. As much as I was loving the feeling of being so intimately in his embrace, I wasn't sure that I was fully ready for the implications here.

"Oh hush, I know. No, that's not why I've brought you here. But I won't tell you I'm not enjoying this wholeheartedly. There's much more you don't know, Bridget, and it's time I've told you. Is it alright if I hold you?"

I looked up at him and he kissed me, just barely at first. Damn it, but I kissed him back and a wave of desire shot through me, and the kiss deepened. It was a few seconds before he pulled away, and I missed him instantly.

"Sorry...I've wanted to do that for a very long time. I shouldn't have."

"No, that's ok," I said breathlessly, shamelessly, still staring at his lips and wondering what the hell we did now. The line's been blurred now, why not blur it some more?

He must've thought the same thing because he kissed me again, putting one giant hand on my rib cage and the other on my neck, further deepening the kiss. My hands were white knuckled in his shirt, pulling him closer to me before I wrapped an arm around him to grab one massive shoulder.

A soft growl emitted from somewhere on the floor, and Declan pulled away again. With mirth in his eyes and a wicked smile on his face he gave me one last peck and sat upright again, settling me back into his side. We did some deep breathing and finally he broke the silence.

"Right, now that we've gotten that out of the way. For now." He winked at me. "It's time I told you why I brought you here."

I just nodded dumbly, still trying to quell my raging hormones and slow my heartbeat. The dog, I'd forgotten all about the dog. Hell, I'd forgotten my own name for a few seconds there. I grabbed the tea mug to keep from attacking him further.

"You know, I never said it was okay," I chided.

His laughter broke the tension.

"Bridget, you know damn well you've wanted that to happen forever too. You can't lie to me."

I rolled my eyes. He wasn't wrong.

"Okay so you have something to tell me?" I said to change the subject.

"The problem is I don't know where to start. All right," he said after a minute. "Bridget, tell me. You noticed the dog was staring at you for months?"

"Animals, babies, and old people love me. I noticed the dog, but it wasn't that weird," I replied, meaning every word of it.

Another reason I didn't want to ruin our relationship with blurring lines. He was about all I had. Dogs and babies loved me, adults not as much. I had lost enough friends and family, and I was terribly short on them to begin with.

"Ah, I know. All right, well when you lose your temper, do odd things happen to those who made you angry?"

"You mean karma?" I said a little snidely. I had a temper to be sure, but I wasn't quick to anger. You had to really smash my buttons to get me to snap.

Then it was of biblical proportions when I finally did. You deserved it if I snapped.

"That's my girl," he said with a wink. He'd earned my ire only once, but he enjoyed getting under my skin. I think it was a love of teasing me, pushing the buttons to see what he could get away with.

"Wait, you're not married are you?" I interjected.

"What?" he said with a laugh.

"Well, you're asking about anger, and I mean look at this place! It's huge, and it's decorated beautifully, and it's clean," I said.

"Oh, love, no. Not married, not yet. Though I'm not opposed to it." He winked at me.

"So why this huge, beautiful house?"

"Well, I've done well for myself. But it's not about me yet. I have a story to tell you."

"But the decorations."

"Do you like it?"

"Well, yes."

"Good, I had them done for you."

"No, you didn't."

"Bridget, yes, I did. I just thought, well, I think quite highly of you. So I had someone come in and make it feel homey for you. It will make more sense when I tell you. Or maybe not, but you do like it, right?" he finished a little flustered, which was very unlike him.

"You're not going to show me a shrine you made of me next, right?"

"God, Bridget, a man tries to be romantic, and you ask if I made a shrine to you?"

Now it was my turn to laugh.

"I mean you could hardly blame me, there're quite a few things you haven't told me apparently."

He rolled his eyes.

"Right, fine. But there is no wife and no shrine. Satisfied?"

"Hardly,"

He kissed me again. Just a firm, quick kiss on my lips but it still set off fireworks.

"How about now?"

"It's a start."

"A start indeed. Now, what do you know of the Tuatha Dé Danann?"

"Not much. Irish, I know, and supernatural, but it was only mentioned in a book I'd read." I read a lot of books.

"And what about Aos Si?"

"Lost me," I replied.

"Well, what if I told you the world was full of supernatural sorts, and you were one of them?"

"It'd explain quite a lot, actually," I answered honestly. I had a weird life.

His deep laugh took me by surprise and when I glanced up at him he started laughing more.

"What?" I said sharply, though I always enjoyed his laughter.

"Here I am thinking you'll be running for the door, and you say, 'why, yes, that makes perfect sense.'"

"Well, isn't that a good thing?" I said suddenly self-conscious.

He gave me another kiss, his body shaking with laughter all the while.

"Yes, love. It is. It just proves to me I've the right of things," he answered.

"I'm not following."

"It's only a hunch. You see, I think I've been looking for you for centuries, only just now remembering it all."

"You're really going to have to elaborate. And it definitely sends 'shrine vibes.'"

"Such a wise ass, that was one thing that tipped me off."

I just raised an eyebrow at him, over the theatrics and far too tired to care about the absurdity of it all. I'd always known there was something different about me, never quite putting my finger on it.

Animals, babies, and the people normal society rejected, they always found their way to me. I wondered whether there was something on my face that tipped them off. An aura that told them "she'll take care of you."

Like a flock of sheep they'd follow me around, not wanting anything other than love and acceptance, and I gave them that.

The rejects, the misunderstood, the sad and lonely, I'd be approached in all manner of places. At the grocery store, at work. People would tell me their whole life story while I listened and nodded.

My bosses preferred I didn't collect them, but they were happy for the business, so they let it go. Good listening skills were a prerequisite to being a good bartender.

My father in particular didn't enjoy it, claiming it was a trait I'd inherited from my mother. I don't think he ever imagined what that said about him.

"Now, I haven't gotten it all figured out yet," he continued. "I only just stumbled upon it myself. But I have enough faith I thought it was time enough I brought it to your attention. This dog here was the most important clue. I've seen my share of wolfhounds, but none like him. I think he's been sent to watch over you."

The dog had done plenty of watching me. It had crossed my mind that he was some sort of sign, but I'd dismissed it. The universe was always sending me signs—some I could make sense of, others not as much.

A cardinal was a loved one visiting me from the spirit world, usually telling me everything was all right. The number thirteen was Saint Anthony, and he was telling me I was protected and to keep going. Lots of big and little things popped up when you paid attention.

Irish wolfhounds like this one were used to protect kings in ancient Ireland. They were huge, fierce in battle, and protective of their masters. Quite literally, they used to hunt wolves and keep the flock of sheep safe. Thus ensuring the safety of the inhabitants of castle and keep.

"I know he's been watching you, only I didn't know why. But us Irish are superstitious folk, and so I thought I'd look into one of my books here. I think he's what you'd call a cú sidh or a faerie dog. The Scottish said they were green, and the Irish said they were black as night, but both say he's a death omen," he said.

"Did you hit your head recently?" I asked him. Though, to be honest, I was superstitious myself. My logical brain said I should run for the hills. But my subconscious brain was starting to wake up a little, and it was sending the signals that he was onto something.

"You know you can't lie to me. I see it in your eyes. You think I'm onto something too. Only question is, who's trying to kill you?"

# CHAPTER 3

"You perhaps?" I said.

"Hush, woman. No, not me,"

"You're clearly the obvious choice. A few screws loose, not entirely honest about who you are, super secretive, from another country. Secretly super-rich but works as a waiter. Decorated his house for a woman he's not involved with. These are all very positive signs that you're the killer."

"Not involved, huh? And could you be a little concerned then if I'm the supposed psycho?" he said back.

"No. If you're the psycho, go for it," I said back.

"If I was the psycho, I might take you up on it. You continue to have no regard for your own person. Loner, here with a psycho— you'd make a perfect victim," he retorted.

"Declan. What would you have me say? You bring me to your home under questionable circumstances to tell me a very far-fetched story, and then tell me this dog you've been talking to, who's not yours, is warning of my impending doom."

"Well, sure, when you say it that way..." he said.

He abruptly got up and strode over to the books lining the wall behind us. Grabbing the first one he touched, he brought it back to me. It was one of the old ones covered in vellum. The illumination was barely there on the cover, but when he started going through the pages, there was still the color that ought to be there. Painted and inscribed by a long-ago monk, probably. Despite myself, I was in awe, itching to touch the book myself.

It wasn't that I didn't trust Declan. It just wasn't a believable story he was pitching to me. If that book didn't have some solid evidence I had to leave.

That book though.

I'd always been obsessed with history. When at museums, I knew you weren't allowed to touch because of the oils on your skin, but I couldn't always help myself. There's a part of me that needed to protect the history, and another that needed to touch something that hands long gone had also touched.

To feel transported to their lives by sharing a relic they'd fashioned themselves with primitive tools thousands of years ago. This book was everything. I could imagine an ancestor of mine had made it himself, long forgotten but his work lived on. His legacy for me to enjoy.

"Look," he said. "The Tuatha Dé Danann are like the kings and queens of the faerie folk. The Aos Si being the faerie folk they reigned over. Cú Sidh over here are the faerie dogs."

He showed me the pictures, beautifully rendered on the delicate pages. The words he spoke were clearly visible on the pages, but the rest was in Old Gaelic.

"While I appreciate the book, I can't read the words Declan," I said exasperated.

"Oh, aye," he said. Rarely did he ever use the word, but he looked at me while he did so. It always got me to chuckle. He always liked to make me smile.

Heading back to the bookshelf he grabbed another tome, this one significantly more modern. Flipping through the pages he placed it on the couch beside me while he remained standing. I began reading through the page he'd left it on. It reiterated a lot of what he'd said already.

"Okay but I'm still not following," I said.

He turned to another page and staring back at me was a figure quite like my own. A short woman was depicted in a simple dress. Long brown hair gently framed her face as she looked down upon sheep and other animals.

In one hand was a staff, in the other a hammer, both arms sporting muscles. Among the animals was an owl on her shoulder. Though her face was only partially visible, it wasn't unlike my own. Dark eyes, full lips, round face. But then, I looked Irish like I ought to. The name at the top was Brigid.

"So by your estimation I'm a faerie princess?" I said sardonically.

"Well, now, I haven't gotten that far yet. Listen *Bridget*," he said with emphasis. "What are the odds little old me from Ireland finds myself bored and in search of adventure and I land here? I waltz into your establishment aiming to grab a bite to eat but I saw you and the dog, so I applied instead? I'm shooting from the hip but there's a little voice in my head telling me I need to protect you."

"What are the odds the little voice is a psychotic episode?"

"Don't jest, I'm really asking you. You feel it too. Not just whatever this is between us, but you've seen the signs. I know you saw the raven the other day at work. And the cockroach in the parking lot tonight," he replied.

He had a point. I hadn't forgotten the death omens I kept seeing. I just didn't know he was paying attention too.

Try as I might, I knew there was something brewing lately. There was a weight to the air, like I was walking through sludge. And I had seen the harbingers of death, slowly closing in.

"My love, I don't know what any of it means. I hope you're not in any danger, but I can't explain it all away. Something drove me to find you and I plan on keeping you now."

My stomach did a little flip at that. Keep me, huh?

"What do you propose we do? You got me to your house and what now? How do you even know you can keep me safe?" I said.

"Oh, I'll keep you safe. Don't worry about that. I don't know what we do from here, but I do know I won't let you out of my sight, so you're staying here. Tomorrow we'll go collect your things. Then I guess we'll figure it out from there."

"And what if I object? What about work? Why do we have to stay here?" I threw that last one, not even believing it myself.

"You don't object so don't fuss unnecessarily," he said.

He was right. He knew me too well.

"We're set to work together almost indefinitely. It was an

agreement I'd made with Joe since the beginning."

"What!?" That one got me a little.

Joe was our boss, an older Italian gentleman who had more hair on his forearms than his head, a big soft belly, and a big soft spot for me. It's not surprising he'd allow Declan to watch over me.

And it made sense why he was always looking at us conspiratorially. I almost felt betrayed, but Lord knows if Joe had asked me first I'd have said of course I don't mind working with Declan all the time.

"I mean it's not in the least bit surprising. Joe sees you as a daughter. And I'm a good match," he said as he winked.

I rolled my eyes. He was, but he didn't need me to boost his ego further.

"And also, the Tuatha Dé Danann are hill folk and since we're in the hills here I figure we're safe. I always feel more alive out in the woods, it's why I chose the mountains in the first place. That its sacred ground isn't surprising. I know you feel it too."

He was right again. I never felt more relaxed than when I was in the mountains. They called to me.

"Why now?" I questioned.

"I'm just following the dogs lead. He seemed to think we should get a move on tonight," he said.

"Have you been watching me leave work from the shadows all this while?" I said with a touch of concern.

"Beautiful, we're usually leaving work together. Tonight my mom wanted to talk, so I was on the phone with her and waiting for you. Then, you were spooked about something tonight and rushing to your car. That's when I noticed the dog rushing toward you."

Believable.

"Listen, we're off tomorrow, so in the morning we'll do some more research and just see what we can find. Are you alright to spend the night? I promise not to harass you. Unless you'd like me to," he said with a wink.

Hot flash.

Without breaking eye contact I said, "I'll stay."

I was either daring him to harass me or warning him not to. Let him make of that what he wished. Because I had no clue right now.

Alright, maybe I did.

"Good. Then let's eat and relax. Enough crazy talk for now. The dog seems to be settled so I guess the coast is clear."

The dog was settled in front of the fire, head on his massive paws, fast asleep. Or at least I thought so. Do faerie dogs sleep?

Declan returned the book to the shelf and settled himself next to me, pulling me closer with one brutish arm. I felt swallowed whole. But I was too tired to keep fighting this *feeling* between us, so I tucked my legs up into his lap and gave him a half hug.

He turned the TV on, put my tea down, and handed me my stew. Taking his own he had to remove his arm from around me to eat, but we stayed intimately close together while we ate in companionable silence.

That was my favorite thing about him. I liked company, but I loved being alone. Declan was the best of both worlds, not always requiring conversation but there if I wanted to talk. It was like being alone without being lonely.

Lost in my thoughts I couldn't pay attention to the TV, so I stared at the stars. It wasn't so difficult to believe that there was a world beyond what we knew when you looked at the stars.

I'm from New Jersey, so we don't get the stars that I know exist in other parts of the world. Where they're not diluted by pollution and competing for brightness with a thousand artificial lights from the city. I've been to places that those stars existed, and I know that what I saw was still only a taste of what they look like in their natural beauty.

Looking at the stars I think you have to believe in magic.

I'd forgotten how hungry I was and before I knew it, there wasn't a drop of stew left. Declan admired my appetite, another thing I appreciated about him. You rarely catch me eating salad unless it's followed by steak or pasta.

Putting my bowl back I finished the last bit of tea that remained and settled firmly into Declan's side. All of the electricity from earlier was a comfortable hum now that I was warm and full. I thought I'd feel weird, and of course it was still new, but somehow it felt right. Like I belonged here. And that was trouble.

He tilted my chin up with one finger under my jaw and gave me a firm kiss on the lips. It wasn't the fire that happened before but a comfortable sizzle.

"Well, lass, there's no two ways about it. I'd like to sleep in my bed and that means you're coming with," he said matter-of-factly.

Just breathe.

"Okay," I said back. I think I said it confidently.

He gathered up our dinner, such as it was, and carted it off to the kitchen. When he returned he had two glasses of water in his hands. I shut the TV off while he put the glasses down and scattered the remaining embers from what was left of the roaring fire.

*I can do this,* I thought. *I'm an adult and so is he and we're just going to go to sleep. It's Declan, don't worry.*

It's Declan, that's why I was worried. I'd almost prefer to go to bed with a stranger than Declan right now. Strangers I could count on to disappear in the morning, never to be remembered again. Except when I judged myself at night, but I did that anyway.

If Declan disappeared, I didn't think I could handle it. And I would definitely remember.

*And what if he stays?* I wasn't really ready for that either.

He grabbed the glasses again and began to lead the way up the stairs. Pine floors and walls made up the stairwell with pictures of strangers hanging here and there.

When we got to the top, there were two hallways, one leading along the balcony overlooking the living room and one headed straight back. All was done in the same pine that the floor was made of, with pictures of nature scenes and people along the walls. We went straight, passing four doors on the left and three on the right. Heading away from the balcony, at the far end he opened the door to his room.

I wondered what was behind the doors on the right, I hadn't ventured that way yet, maybe an office. The doors were all closed but two were clearly closets and one a bathroom I assumed. Which made me think four were bedrooms. Why does he have a five-plus bedroom house anyway?

Walking into the bedroom there were more pinewood floors and walls, with a plush black rug under the biggest bed I'd ever seen. Above the bed was a giant skylight, showcasing the stars above. But that wasn't even the best part,.

To the right of the bed was a huge bay window complete with a bench seat with gray cushions. Like the balcony one but bigger and infinitely cozier tucked away in the bedroom.

Beyond the bay window was a small lake, the mountains beyond, and all the stars that shone in between. The moon reflected off the surface of the lake, looking like glass, pitch black and inky except where the moon shone.

I walked directly to the window and sat on the bench, basking in the beauty for a few moments. Declan came up behind me and put his hands on my shoulders.

"I agree," was all he said.

"I didn't know there was a lake out here."

"Yeah, it's not well known."

"Shame, it's beautiful."

"Thanks, it's mine," he responded.

"Your lake?"

"Yes, mine. To be succinct, my family had money, and I didn't waste the opportunity I'd been given. I've built mostly internet companies and sold them, invested the rest, and this is essentially my retirement," he said flippantly.

"So you're also a vampire?" I said looking at him. I mean he couldn't be more than thirty. How was he retired already?

He laughed, catching my meaning. "No, but I'll bite if you'd like me to," he said with a wink.

I didn't have an answer for that, well a verbal answer. I bit my lip to keep from doing anything erratic. Like undoing his belt.

*You're hopeless.* I chided myself for having no self-control.

He walked back to the bathroom that was attached and I was grateful to be left alone for a moment. The view was breathtaking, and I was thanking the stars above that Declan had found his way to me. No matter the circumstances, he was a welcome reprieve from what I was accustomed to.

Even if he turned out to be a psycho, at least he had a nice house. And one night in a bed like this was probably worth the cost. Well, with Declan at least.

I wasn't particularly lucky in love, and less in life. I'd grown up in middle class suburbia, a small town where everyone knew everyone's business. Hard to hide in a small town like that.

So while I tried to keep up appearances, the chaos of my home life inevitably leaked out into my daily life. Getting involved with the less desirable crowd because they accepted me and vice versa. We had shared pain.

And then in comes Declan. All tall and lean but built like a brick wall. Million-dollar smile, maybe literally.

You can't afford things like this in New Jersey unless you had money. And I don't care where in the world this house was, it cost money. Not the kind of money I had.

Suddenly feeling dejected and unworthy (again), I took one last long look out the window. There was a black figure out by the lake that I thought looked like a seal. *Great now the Loch Ness monster is in the lake,* I thought.

Dismissing my imagination and shaking off my pity-party I turned to see Declan watching me. Great.

Taking two long strides he pulled me into his arms and gave me a solid squeeze.

"Don't worry so much," he said. "Now go get comfortable so we can sleep."

"Quit watching me all the time."

"Quit getting lost in your head and I won't have the opportunity."

I rolled my eyes at him. At least our relationship hadn't

changed much, yet.

Taking his direction I went to the bathroom and swished some mouthwash in my mouth I found in his cabinet. The bathroom was immaculate too, of course. All marble like the kitchen, with a separate portion for a shower behind a wall of marble, separate jetted tub, and a double sink. Ah, the life of luxury. I'd enjoy it while I could.

Exiting the bathroom I suddenly felt very self-conscious as I made my way to the bed. I was self-conscious often, but not usually in this arena. I've found that men aren't that complicated in the bedroom. The goal was clear and defined. That I could handle.

But something about getting into bed with Declan was very different from the other men in my life. Something monumental, like I was at the precipice, and I would either fall to my demise or learn to fly.

Declan was already lying down, one arm behind his head, the other flipping through channels on the TV. I crawled in and it felt like a cloud. I instantly groaned. My aching muscles appreciated this so much.

"Sore? I could help." He raised his eyebrows at me.

I scoffed. Too tired to tease now that I was so comfortable.

"Does the TV bother you? I think I need something to soothe my nerves tonight," he asked.

"No, I think I do too. Thanks."

Putting the remote down he reached over and pulled me to him. Settling my head on his chest and laying a hand on one pec, I was sucked into a deep sleep much quicker than I'd hoped.

# CHAPTER 4

I woke up hot and slightly squished. Someone was wrapped around me, and it took me a few moments to orient myself. Declan was beside me; I'd woken up to worse. The bright blue sky was directly above me, telling me it was later than it felt. It felt like I just closed my eyes but that was hours ago.

Declan stirred beside me, squeezing me more. I snuggled closer, enjoying waking up beside him. What a difference a few hours can make.

I thought Declan was attractive. I just never imagined us being a thing. There weren't fireworks when we just hung out after work, but it was comfortable and relaxed. I mean, there was always a current of electricity between us, but it was usually set to dim.

We had numerous topics we could talk about, more than I could say for anyone else I'd ever met. Even my best friend from my childhood, I couldn't say we had a ton to talk about. We talked about shared experiences or shared acquaintances, but we didn't have a ton in common.

Maybe that was why I simply didn't explore the more than friends avenue with Declan. He was too valuable as a friend.

Well, that and I didn't think I was worthy of someone like Declan but that's another story. Why was he interested in me anyway? Was he interested in me?

He didn't even try to take my clothes off last night, so maybe he's not that into me. I mean, he's never tried to get me in bed in the past. But then why the kisses? I wasn't making up our chemistry. Surely that kind of fireworks couldn't be one-sided?

There was no going back now. We were exploring this, or we were parting ways. Only, where would we go from here? I blanched at the idea.

Having had no successful long-term relationships to this point I dreaded the notion that by this time next year I'd be without Declan and therefore without a friend again. But there was only one way to know for sure wasn't there?

I just wondered what he thought about all of this. He'd said a few things last night that made me think that he'd thought more about kissing me than he'd previously led me to believe.

"What are you blathering on about over there?" His sleepy voice said suddenly.

I put my hand to my mouth. Had I said some of that aloud?

"No, you haven't said it out loud, but I can *feel* it. For the record, I didn't plan on kissing you either. Well, I never objected to it, of course, and there were times I wanted to. I just wasn't looking for a relationship at this point in time. Then I kissed you and I didn't know just how much I'd like it until I did it. I think I only decided I absolutely needed to when you crash-landed into me. Then I wondered why it had taken me so long to realize I wanted to."

I glanced over at him. That about summed it up.

"I don't know what to do about it either. I figure we'll find that out together though, won't we?" he said softly.

At that I leaned over to press my lips gently to his, testing the waters. I liked it more than I thought I would because my hands fisted into his shirt as I pulled him closer for another.

Not wanting to ruin the magic I pulled back after that one, a little breathless.

"I suppose we will," I whispered.

"I'll get the coffee started," he said giving me a peck on the forehead before throwing the sheets off himself and heading for the stairs. "Eggs for breakfast?"

"Yes, please," I said back.

As I sat and waited for my body to will itself into action, I thought about all he'd said last night. Some obvious signs had popped up lately, all death omens. All could be explained away but the damn dog.

Finally getting up I went over to the bay window. Staring out at the lake with clear eyes this morning I wondered again about the figure I saw out there last night. Sometimes in the fog of exhaustion, your mind plays tricks on you.

Other times you see things you weren't meant to see, only your mind wasn't closed off to the possibility. I wondered which was true in this case.

The view was truly spectacular, and I was hesitant to leave it. Only, I didn't want to press my luck. Staying in Declan's bedroom all day was a can of worms I wasn't ready to open. My body might be, but my brain wasn't. My heart decided it wasn't touching that with a ten-foot pole.

The smell of coffee, fire, and bacon met me as I made my way down the hall to the stairs. I couldn't think of a much better smell to wake up to.

Rounding the corner of the stairs into the dining room I saw that he'd set two places next to each other at the end of the long table, closest to the window. Searching for Declan, I saw him at the stove with his back to me. I decided I liked the view here too.

Coming up behind him I put my hand on his lower back like usual. The restaurant custom is to shout, "Behind you," anytime you're behind a coworker in the kitchen.

This is so they don't knock whatever you're carrying out of your hands or vice versa. I'm generally too quiet for people to hear so when I had my hands free I tended to touch people instead. Or politely shove them if I was busy.

Hard muscles met my hand and inappropriate thoughts flooded my mind. If I'm being honest, that wasn't relatively new. But it had a whole new meaning now.

Removing my hand I said, "Can I help?"

"Make the coffee and bring it into the other room for me?" he said.

"Sure thing," I answered.

Already knowing how he took his coffee from work I set

about my task. Opening his fridge for the milk I was pleasantly surprised to see it filled with food. For some reason, I thought he'd have the bachelor kind of fridge with only condiments. Well, after I got over the idea he was married.

Food was evidence that maybe he cooked regularly, a good sign when you wanted to date an adult and not just a giant child. I was still looking for reasons to not go down this path with him, but I was coming up empty.

Bringing the coffee to the table I sat and enjoyed the view again from a different angle than the bedroom. With more trees over here, I could feel the magic that was in the woods. They were the best early in the morning and when the sun went down. The magic felt strongest then.

Declan placed my food in front of me and sat opposite me with his own. Bacon egg and cheese on toast, a favorite of mine.

A small smile formed on his lips, but his eyes were sad.

"What's wrong?" I asked.

"Can't help but wonder why you aren't here under normal circumstances."

"What difference does it make?"

"Well, why haven't I thought to ask you on a date? It's not like I wasn't attracted to you from the start. And a date is the way it should have started, but I chickened out. Why now? I had to kidnap you to get you here. It doesn't sit right with me."

"What an ego boost."

"Well, that's precisely what I mean."

"I don't know Declan, maybe it wouldn't have worked if we weren't friends first. Maybe if you'd taken me on a date, I would've screwed it up." *Maybe I'll still screw it up.*

Maybe I had to trust you first to even let you close to me. If we went on a date, you'd be like all the rest.

He saw the meaning in my eyes though because after a beat his eyes turned sober before the mischief returned and the smile broadened.

"Yeah, I'm sure you have the right of it. You definitely would have screwed it up." He winked at me on that one. "Besides, kidnapping you adds a lot of flair to the story. 'Oh, how'd you two get together?' 'Well I kidnapped her and then our romance blossomed.'"

He took my issues in stride.

"If that's even what this is yet," I said back.

He just grunted at me.

Yeah, I knew it too. There was no more going back.

Taking a bite of food I was feeling more like this could be a thing after all.

"Well, if you cook everything as well as these eggs I suppose I could keep you around."

"Oh, so that's all you need me for?" He winked again and my stomach flip-flopped.

Blushing into my plate I suddenly was worried about the dog. Where the hell was he anyway? Don't they usually beg for food?

"Where's the dog?" I asked.

"Let him out, he hasn't returned yet."

"Should we be worried?"

"I don't think so."

"Should we name him?"

"Probably. Any suggestions?"

"None, you?"

"I think Sid, Cu Sidh, Sid."

"Works for me."

Finishing breakfast in comfortable silence, I gathered the empty plates, put them in the dishwasher, and got us two more cups of coffee.

"So what's the first order of business?" I said as I sat back down.

"Well, I figure I'll shower and get ready here. You're welcome to as well unless you'd rather wait, and we'll go to your place, and you can shower there if you want. Then I was thinking we could check out a few libraries. I have plenty of books here for when we're back but there might be some I don't own that could give us a few clues."

"Yeah, I think that's a fine plan. I'll opt to shower at my place."

So I could shave my legs and look somewhat presentable.

Looking like he knew my private thoughts again he took his coffee and got up.

"Well, I won't be long. If you change your mind, you know where to find me," he said as he kissed me on the cheek.

"Hmm," I said back. I probably would have if I felt more presentable in all honesty. Hence the shower at home.

Deciding I'd rather sit and enjoy my coffee by the fire I got up and made my way to the living room. The giant glass wall was breathtaking, with all tall green trees and blue sky. On my way, I saw the dog out on the deck and let him in.

"Hey, Sid," I said.

He gave me a disgruntled look. Maybe he didn't like the name we'd chosen. Too bad. If he was a faerie dog, he could tell me his name when he was ready. If not, Sid it was.

I sat on the couch to wait for Declan to finish up, pulling out my phone and checking my emails. I'm forever astonished at the sheer volume of junk mail that accumulates. Some of them I'm certain I've unsubscribed to before, yet there they are week after week.

After a while, there was a loud thump on the glass and I looked up, startled. A few feathers were floating in the air, long and black.

I got up to investigate. It's not odd for birds to fly into glass but I hated the idea that he might be out there and hurt. Peeking out the door onto the deck I saw the poor thing motionless.

Heading back inside I grabbed my dirty work shirt from last night. I have three others the same as this one if it got ruined. I brought the shirt outside to wrap around the bird, closing Sid inside so he didn't try to eat the poor thing. But when I looked it was gone. Maybe it had only stunned itself.

I looked around for a minute and decided it had flown away, so I grabbed the door to go back inside.

Something wet and squishy sounding slapped my midsection, knocking me down. When I picked my head up it was the seal, I think.

The tail and body were like a seal, but I'd never seen a human-looking head on a seal before. She was a murky sea green, with wild green hair that flowed around her face like she was still underwater. Her green eyes were more like a snake than a human eye and her teeth were fangs.

The loudest howl I'd ever heard came from the living room and the seal creature turned its head. It looked terrified. When it swiveled its head back to me, the door opened and out came Sid and Declan.

In an instant, the seal creature was gone. I don't remember it leaving but Sid was racing off for the water. Declan was at my side trying to get my attention, bare-chested and barefoot.

Tattoos I didn't previously know existed snaked all across his torso and arms. Damn it, he was good-looking.

"What the hell was that?" I said to him.

"Well, if you ask me it was a selkie. Are you all right? It didn't hurt you did it?" he replied.

"Yeah, I think I'm fine, it only knocked me down. What are selkies?" I asked.

"They're mermaids of a sort. Faerie folk that are part human and part seal,"

"And you know this, how?"

"I grew up in Ireland, silly. These are the stories you hear. You have your local legends, the Jersey Devil and the sort. We have faeries. And my mom is a bit superstitious. Now shush, let's go inside. Before the Jersey Devil shows up next."

"Unlikely since he lives in the Pine Barrens down in South Jersey," I retorted, allowing Declan to pull me to my feet.

The trouble was he was shirtless, and I was doing my damndest not to stare. Or touch. The tattoos took it to another level of hotness that made me suddenly very glad for my current situation.

As he ushered me inside, I took some deep breaths to calm my raging hormones. A combination of desire and adrenaline coursed through my veins, and I was having trouble wrangling them into submission.

I saw different Celtic knots, words, and other ominous-looking tattoos that I wanted to ask about, but I guess would have to wait. Only because right now speech was hard to come by.

Sid came back in behind Declan, with a menacing scowl etched on his face. His tail was low, and he stalked in, very unhappy with the mornings' events. He must not have gotten the creature.

I was still wearing Declan's clothes but now they were wet with patches of slime on them. Giving myself a once over, I couldn't see anything else had happened to me. I guess Sid saved the day, giving Declan a warning to come out there.

"So what do you suppose that was all about?" I asked.

"I really couldn't say. I know what selkies are; they're mermaids. Beautiful half-fish women that lure sailors to their death. None of that is true here—no sailors and it wasn't pretty."

"I thought you said that we were safe here?"

"I said the mountains are where the magic is. Lots of magic for all sorts of faerie folk too, apparently. But we're safe aren't we?"

Sort of. "I saw that thing last night out by the lake. I just assumed I was imagining things."

"Well, how about next time you imagine things you let me know? And don't go outside by yourself. At least bring Sid here with you. Why were you out there anyway?"

"A raven had flown into the glass. I had gotten my work shirt and was going to pick it up and check that it wasn't injured. Only when I got outside again with the shirt it was gone and then that thing got me." Where was my shirt now anyway?

"Where is your shirt now?" Declan echoed my thoughts.

"That's a good question."

Declan went over to the door and peered out, looking left and right. He came back in still shirtless himself and without my shirt.

"Don't see it," he said.

More mysteries, still no answers.

"Not a big deal. I have more," I said more to comfort myself.

Had that thing taken my shirt? Why?

"Yeah, huh, well, you look a mess and since I have more clothes, why don't you shower here before we go to your place?"

"Yeah, I might as well." Looking down at myself I didn't want to get in my car with this gunk on me. Except then I couldn't shave, and I had no underwear or bra to put on, both wet from the mermaid.

Oh well, I'd survive. That is, if I didn't spontaneously combust first. Being near a shirtless Declan thinking about my lack of clothing was playing with fire. A shower was definitely in order.

He led the way to his bedroom and his private bathroom and got a towel from the closet for me. He went behind the wall for the shower, starting the water.

Heading back to the bedroom he got together some clothes for me. Gray sweatpants and a black sweatshirt promoting some gym in red letters.

Putting them on the vanity for me he asked, "Is there anything else you need?"

His eyes smoldered, his voice deep and husky. Ugh, he was trouble.

"No thanks, Declan," I said breathlessly. Breath was hard to come by suddenly and my whole body tensed up. I was trying not to throw myself at him, but I was starting to think that it was a fine idea. It's inevitable, I told myself, why not now?

He kissed me then, slowly and softly. One hand cupping my neck, the other holding my waist firmly. I didn't want to dirty his clean clothes, so I laid my hands on his stomach to keep my clothes from touching his.

Hard abs met my touch, dusted with reddish hair, and I couldn't figure out if I wanted to make my hands go up or down to explore. I left them firmly in place, not trusting myself at all.

"Right then," he said as he pulled away. "I'll leave you to it." And he left the bathroom and closed to door.

It took me a moment before returning to earth. When I did I shook my head in exasperation. What the hell man? I don't know what was more unbelievable—kissing Declan or faeries out to get me.

Peeling off Declan's clothes, off of my body unfortunately and not his, I jumped in the shower. More like walked into the shower. I'd never used one like this and was wondering how he'd turned it on without getting wet himself.

It was spacious behind the wall, enough to fit him and me and still have room. Banishing that thought immediately I saw that he'd turned the shower to face the wall. Testing the water I noticed there were extra shower heads built into the sides of the wall and there was a separate knob for them underneath the main knob.

Feeling insignificant again I started going through reasons why I should put an end to this tryst before it got started. I didn't feel worthy of all this luxury, and even less worthy of his attention. He'd been a perfect gentleman to this point.

What was wrong with him? There had to be something.

Spending most of the shower finding reasons to put an end to this relationship we'd been forming, I exited feeling pretty down and out. I didn't have time or patience for a relationship.

And besides, I hadn't had a successful one to date so what's the point? I hated wasting time getting to know someone and then they were gone.

Getting dressed, I decided. That was it—no more kisses, no more snuggling, no getting close to him at all. I'd sleep on the couch tonight if he insisted. Sid would keep me plenty safe.

Exiting the bathroom, Declan was sitting at the bench seat in the window with his laptop in front of him and his phone to his ear. He looked severe, his presence formidable, a deep scowl on his face.

"Make it happen," he said and hung up the phone.

Damn it. I was a goner.

Feeling like I wanted him to throw me on the bed and have his way with me until his frown turned upside down I took a step closer into the room. When he saw me he looked like he might like that idea too.

"What's up?" I said. How lame.

"I'm upping my security here. There are a few blind spots I'd like squared away. The problem is they can't come until tomorrow. Which means I'll have to keep you extra close for the next twenty-four hours," he said. He said the last words with a huskiness that showed that he'd picked up on my thoughts exactly.

Closing his laptop and striding over to me he had me in his arms in moments. Kissing me with an urgency he hadn't expressed yet, he grabbed my ass and pulled me closer. God but I didn't even have any bra or underwear on, and his clothes fit so loose, there was very little in the way.

Ending the kiss but still holding me close he said, "Bridget, I don't mean to keep at you like this, but I can't seem to help myself anymore. I need to know if it's all right."

Damn it. All the reasons I thought of for why we had to end this were completely forgotten. I couldn't help myself either.

"It's all right," I said back.

"Only all right?" he responded with a wicked grin as he kissed me again, picking me up by my behind as I wrapped my legs around him.

"Only all right," I panted.

He laid me down on the bed, leaning over me, my legs still wrapped around his waist. He said, "I'll show you alright," with a growl.

Continuing his assault of my senses we ran our hands all over each other. He was large, everywhere.

With a groan, we both pulled back from each other. This was dangerous territory. His face still only inches from mine he kissed me more gently a few times, hands framing my face.

"Yeah," I said on an exhale. Truth be told, I would be more than happy to continue but it didn't seem to be the time.

I still wasn't sure if he was insane or not, and we really ought to get a move on if I was to be gathering my things at home and heading to the library. It was practically lunchtime now too, so we'd probably have to bring something to eat in the car.

Besides, the anticipation made it more exciting.

"You might make an honest man outta me yet," he breathed.

"You might be the death of me yet," I answered with a huff.

With one last kiss, he got up and pulled me to my feet.

"I'd prefer you alive a while longer if that's ok," he said pointedly.

"Yeah that sounds pretty good to me too," I answered honestly.

The reminder of my supposed demise sufficiently snuffed out the flames that threatened to consume us. That's why I was here after all, not for a roll in the hay.

Or, not only for a roll in the hay. I find I quite like the idea of rolling around with Declan now.

Walking down the hallway he said, "So how did I do?"

"You're a solid four," I answered.

"Out of five, I hope."

"No, out of ten," I said with a smirk.

His answer was to smack my butt.

"You keep your four, I won't be kissing you anymore," he said.

"Hmm, fine with me," I said.

Truthfully, I don't think I'd be fine with it, but he didn't have to know that. And besides, he was only playing to keep the mood light. Things felt a little too heavy suddenly.

As I followed him down the hall, I remembered my grandmother always telling me to marry my best friend. At the time I had thought of my best friend and thought *him*?

My best friend throughout my high school years was Jared, and as much as we got along, I never felt any romantic feelings toward him. We'd drifted apart after high school a bit, each falling into different routines and with different crowds, but if I texted him he usually answered.

Truthfully, I missed him, but my lack of romantic feelings was a part of our drifting apart. That and I had gotten out of the life Jared was still currently in, and it would do me more harm to be around him. But I still considered him my best friend.

Besides Declan, but then, can I qualify Declan as my best friend now? Or my boyfriend?

Joking around with Declan felt like what my grandmother

had truly meant. The camaraderie, knowing what the other was thinking, picking up where the other one was falling behind, yin and yang. This felt a little more like falling in love with your best friend.

Shit. Was I falling in love with Declan!? Alarm bells started ringing again. Messing around with Declan would be one thing, but here I am already thinking I couldn't bear it if he didn't kiss me every chance he got. Trouble. I was in a lot of trouble.

He grabbed my hand when we got to the living room and squeezed it. Continuing into the dining room to the kitchen he asked, "Sandwiches fine?"

"Yeah, thanks," I said back. I was starving actually.

While we made sandwiches, him taking things and putting them on the island, me assembling my sandwich, and him his I thought of how domesticated this all was. It is the little things, isn't it? Our level of comfortability extended to his house easily, and I was enjoying it.

He gave Sid some food in a bowl and got a bowl of water to go with. Something I was sad I hadn't thought to do until now. I guess I didn't think a faerie dog needed things like this.

"I gave him something last night too while you changed. He was fine. And I figure this morning he took care of himself," Declan said.

"I didn't think of it. I'm not even sure he needs to eat."

"To be honest, neither am I but I figured we ought to all the same."

"Yeah, I agree. Ready?"

"Let's do it. I think we ought to stop at a pet store too, now you mention it. We can't be walking around with a giant dog without a leash, and he really ought to eat dog food, I think," Declan answered.

"Yeah, I suppose you're right," I said. A faerie dog on a leash... how absurd was that?

We all headed out into the garage and got in my car. Declan gave me directions to get back to my apartment but otherwise, we didn't talk much. Too much on our minds for it.

# CHAPTER 5

Pulling in front of my apartment felt odd for some reason. It was as if one night at Declan's and this tiny little apartment was no longer my home. It felt cold and isolated, where Declan's felt full of life. And possibly love.

Or maybe it was just that he had every luxury one could buy so I was feeling how much this apartment lacked. I wasn't a gold digger, but I also wasn't an idiot. Money can't buy happiness, but it does afford some things that can make one pretty content.

My apartment was red brick, two floors with one apartment above the other. A communal main door that led directly to the two different apartment doors.

Mostly the shared landing was just for the mail. The apartments were connected to two just like them and each building housed maybe a dozen apartments.

This complex wasn't huge, maybe two suburban blocks worth. But I could park directly in front of my apartment and carrying groceries in wasn't a problem.

There was a laundry facility a few buildings over. I've tried to carry my laundry there before but it's usually more a pain than anything, so I'll drive it over. I am from New Jersey.

It's a no-frills type of place, utilitarian with only the necessities. There was no dishwasher, no balcony, no complaints. Occupants were hard-knock people for a hard-knock life.

Everyone watched out for each other and chipped in to help if they could, without getting overly involved. I'd never had a real reason to complain about it. My main wish was to have a washer and dryer in the unit. It would make life so much easier and cleaner.

Declan had been here countless times with me. To bullshit after work and wind down, watch a movie, devour pizza. It didn't matter to me before what my apartment was like but now that I knew where he lived I felt some type of way about it.

Maybe I was just contemplating being naked around Declan in tight quarters. But it was still a lot of feelings of lack. Why would he want to be with me? I kept circling back around to this question.

Clearing my head of silly thoughts I led the charge inside. Declan grabbed my hand before I started up the stairs. He kept doing things like that and I liked it more than I was willing to admit.

"Let me go first in case there's anything amiss," he said.

Chivalry is not dead after all. Moving past me in the small stairwell I realized again how big he was. He was like a Clydesdale of human beings, just unbelievably bigger than you think things ought to be. Well, at least little old me thought so.

Not that I was complaining about his size, quite the contrary.

He walked through all of the apartment, throwing back the shower curtain, opening the closet doors. Nothing was out of sorts.

"What would you have done if something was here?" I questioned.

"Cross that bridge when I got to it. That's your problem, love. You can't plan for life that way," he said.

"You could've brought the bat," I said as I showed him the baseball bat in my hand that I left near the front door. It wasn't entirely necessary. It was a safe neighborhood. Like super safe. But I had that for the same reason you keep feminine products in your purse. Just in case.

He took the bat and smacked my rear with it.

"Smart ass," he said as he brushed a kiss on my lips.

I was enjoying those kisses too much. I'd say stupid things all day if he kept kissing me for it.

He settled himself on the couch and turned the TV on while

I started packing things. The trouble with packing things is you can make a case for anything you want to. Do I need a curling iron? Of course not. But what if I wanted to look super sexy one of these nights?

I always packed everything but the kitchen sink and then went through the bag another time or two to condense. Not the quickest or easiest way to do it, and I always made a bigger mess than anything, but it worked. Call it deductive reasoning but my brain worked better backward than forward sometimes.

Finally settled with one of my camping backpacks and a purse filled with essentials, I took a quick shower. I did want to shave, and Declan didn't have shampoo and conditioner like my hair needed. Getting dressed in jeans, boots, and a thermal I felt decent.

The problem was that we didn't know how long I'd be staying there so I wanted to have enough to last awhile without practically moving in. I was fairly certain Declan had a washer and dryer at his house though so what I had ought to do.

Putting on thick socks in my bedroom and pulling on my best boots I chanced a glance in the mirror. I looked fine, but I decided to go ahead and add some mascara for courage. It couldn't hurt to feel a little courageous.

"All right, I guess I'm good," I said.

I was somewhat grateful for no funny business in my apartment. Everything felt too real, surrounded by my personal effects and memories we had shared here. As if we did it at his mansion it could be a dream, but here it would be very real.

It was funny to think of how much trust I had put in him from the start. As if on sight we had understood the other.

Funny how hindsight is twenty/twenty. Most other people never understood me. Even after years of knowing me I had to explain myself all the time, questioning my intentions and assuming the worst of me.

As a general rule of thumb where I was concerned, I didn't care that much. I'm too busy having conversations with myself in my head. I don't have time to plan horrendous things to do to anyone else. Nor would I if I did. I'm a very live and let live kind of person.

Things were rarely complicated where Declan and I were concerned. He never misinterpreted my signals, wouldn't dream of thinking I was out to get him, and took my depression and anxiety for what it was. A reflection of my life experiences, not a knock on him. Sometimes you just click, I suppose.

If you ask me, most people miss the subtle cues that Declan and I understood. The intent behind words and actions.

Most of the time people get hung up in the arbitrary. That's why many people find me to be too blunt. Everyone else gets caught up in making things pretty, but I prefer to get to the heart of the matter quickly. And with some sarcasm added in for good measure.

In fact, the first time Declan came over we'd been sitting in the parking lot after work talking about exactly that. Not so much our connection but griping about customers not getting to the point.

Someone had complained about their meal but all attempts at appeasing them were insufficient. After a few of the usual first attempts, Declan had exclaimed, "Well what do you want then?"

To which the customer said that they would like it taken off of the bill they'd decided, even though that was one of Declan's suggestions that they had shot down. We'd spent the better part of an hour griping about customers' requests.

The table that says they want nothing when you ask them and then two minutes later they're flagging you down while your boss is watching. Prompting the boss to ask you why you weren't paying attention to your table.

Or the ones that ask for one item at a time, making you run back and forth numerous times like you needed the workout. Even though you always ask, "Can I get you anything else?" before you leave the table.

It's the usual conversation among restaurant workers, a good ice breaker for getting to know the new server or cook. Although the conversation with the new cook is usually the server explaining why they made him remake a Bolognese and it was still taken off the bill. Lots of expletives are usually involved.

I don't know what made me do it, but I had asked him if he wanted to go to my place to continue the conversation. It was summer, and the night was a balmy eighty degrees as summer nights can get in New Jersey.

I read somewhere that our climate was now subtropical. Getting less snow every year, more rain, and humidity so thick your lungs feel like they're filled with soup.

We had sat and continued to sweat for a while before I had enough I think. My apartment is the only logical place because most other things are closed when you get out of work as late as we typically did. And I didn't go to bars anymore.

He had agreed readily, but I never got the twinge of fear or otherwise from inviting a relative stranger into my home. A strange man at that, who was considerably larger than me.

I wasn't prone to being afraid, believing in my abilities to take care of myself. But I always trusted my gut. My gut said Declan was good people and so far so good.

I think we talked clear until 3 am, having gotten out of work around midnight, and gotten to my apartment around 1 am. We continued that routine nearly every night unless we got out extra late or were too tired.

The conversations ranged from work to philosophy and everything in between. We watched TV shows, movies, documentaries, we even read the same books like our own private book club.

But never had we kissed or held hands or thought about it until now. Maybe that's not exactly true. I think we both acknowledged the attraction and chose to ignore it.

I wonder what made him so jaded. We didn't discuss ourselves much, choosing instead to discuss ideas and debate ideologies. Maybe he was running from a past he had no love for.

I knew what pain I left in the past, but what was he hiding?

I wonder if he'd been more interested in me than he'd let me believe. Did he read the *Game of Thrones* with me because he enjoyed it too or was it just to get closer to me? Maybe it wasn't so cut and dry. Perhaps it was always a bit of both.

I thought of all of this as we gathered items and placed them in my car. Leaving a light on in my apartment so it seemed as if someone was home, I wrote a note to my neighbors below me that I would be away for a bit, and I halted my mail delivery. If it was urgent, I was reachable by email or phone.

Lastly, I took the garbage and locked up, effectively moving in with Declan for an indeterminate amount of time. It felt like a natural next step despite my fear. Like all of this time we'd been living at my place but now we were taking a step forward in our time together.

Declan grabbed the garbage from me and went to throw it out. While I sat and waited in my car for him, it really wasn't worth driving over, a raven landed on the hood of my car. This was the third one this week I think.

The curious part of it was that Sid didn't bark at him or anything. I wondered what that meant while Declan came to the car and the raven flew away.

He got in and just gave me a look, silently confirming that he had seen the bird as well. We stayed silent while I drove over to the library. It was closer than the pet store and it closed sooner.

Since we were both nerds, naturally we already had library cards.

"I'll search history since I'm already more familiar with it and you go for mythology," Declan said.

"Yeah, that works," I answered.

We headed in and went our separate ways.

✳ ✳ ✳

After an hour or so I was seeing double, but I had a notebook full of information. The smaller books I skimmed through, and I would check out the bigger ones. I was feeling a little uneasy about some of the information I'd read. With all of the Gaelic words, it took triple the effort to understand sometimes, learning the new words as I went.

I agreed that a lot of the things in there made it seem like I could be Brigid reincarnated or something. A lot of traits of mine were similar. I was hung up on this whole reincarnation part though.

Animals being depicted with pictures of Brigid lent to the belief that she was the goddess of domesticated animals. She was also the goddess of the wayward and children. Specifically, children that were abused or from unhappy families. Sounded familiar so far.

Possibly a triple deity she's said to have two sisters, Brigid the healer and Brigid the smith. Less familiar. I didn't make knives in my spare time.

Her other associations were with poetry, wisdom, healing, and protection. Proposed to also be reminiscent of the British Celtic Goddess Brigantia, depicted alongside Minerva, Victoria, and Tyche/Fortuna.

She was a queen of the Tuatha Dé Danann, wife to Bres, the king. That's what had me nervous. Bres, or Eochu Bres, was purported to be an unpopular king.

With his name meaning "beautiful horseman," one story states that he favored his lineage and clansmen, the Fomorians, and abused the rest. The story said that he was a terrible host and was made to eat poison for his treatment of guests he was supposed to honor.

Bres possibly being misinterpreted and not "beautiful horseman," but "fight" or "blow". So he was probably a narcissist, all pretty words and then stabs you in the back.

Another tale however depicts him as the "flower of Tuatha," and tells of his kindness, noble manner, and his many talents. Both accounts refer to him as the husband of Brigid.

I sure hope this didn't mean Declan.

Brigid's father is Dagda, who is portrayed as the father figure, an important king to the Tuatha. Possessing powers of agriculture, controlling the weather, fertility, magic, wisdom, and

Druidry, he was an exalted member of mythology. Controlling life and death, he was similar to the Norse All-Father, Odin.

Bres' parentage was alarming. The son of Eri of the Tuatha Dé Danann and the Goddess of Ireland through which the country inherited the name and either Prince Elatha ("prince of darkness") of the Fomorians of Balor of the Evil Eye. Bres was described as being twice the size of children his age, looking fourteen while only seven.

The Fomorians being another supernatural race in Ireland, described as hostile and monstrous, were the first inhabitants of Ireland and the enemies of the Tuatha Dé Danann. And sounding like Declan's formidable size.

Often intermarrying with each other, Brigid and Bres' were probably an attempt at uniting the enemy forces. The Fomorians likened to the jötnar of Norse mythology, Bres would be the equivalent of their Loki. Hence the conflicting accounts of his character.

I recounted all of this to Declan in the car, sharing our findings on the way to the pet store. As I drove and stared decidedly at the windshield, I could feel the tension from Declan. If I was Brigid, he was Bres, or at least that's what I had surmised. So what was he, kind and noble, or a trickster?

"I'm following your lead, lass, and I don't like it," he said.

"Well, you tell me," I said shortly.

Apparently, there was also a Saint Bridget, a nun. I could feel his smile.

I was no nun, but it did mean that he didn't have to be Bres.

He continued to tell me that she was a spitfire. Wanting to open a nunnery she had asked the man in charge for a plot of land. The man said sure, however much land you can cover with your shawl.

He didn't anticipate Bridget cutting her shawl into four pieces and telling her fellow nuns to run into four different directions with it, thus granting her a significantly larger share of land.

Tales of her sarcasm, wit, and generosity made me feel a little better about the situation. But it was all the more perplexing.

"What does this mean though?" I asked him.

"I don't know," he said in a huff. "Do you believe in reincarnation?"

"Not particularly, but it doesn't have to be that I'm her, does it?"

"Here's my theory, since you're no nun," he said with a wink. "Maybe you're just more the Aos Si type? Like the general faery sort, and you just have a lot of her traits because you're named after her."

That actually made a fair amount of sense, as far as these things went.

"Like Native American's naming their children after what they were like. Sitting Bull and that sort of thing," I said.

"Yeah, except nowadays you name your children at birth because infant mortality rates aren't what they were. Your mom seems the sort that she might be more connected to the spirit world herself. It's like an 'if you're open to it' sort of thing."

We'd discussed enough philosophy and science for me to get the gist of what he meant. It's like looking around the room for something red. Once I said it you'd find a ton of red things you didn't see before.

Seeing ghosts, believing in the paranormal, and other weird things means maybe you see things other people don't because you're open to the possibility that they exist.

Or your brain makes shit up to accommodate that belief, and you're seeing nonsense and calling it ghosts. Both are equally possible.

It's the placebo effect. The test subjects with the sugar pill have lost their symptoms because they believe it. They really lost them, but it wasn't because of the medicine.

"But the death omens?" I questioned.

"That I haven't been able to figure out. Or the ravens. Interestingly though, I don't suppose you know the name of the first woman to be hanged for witchcraft in Salem do you?"

"It wouldn't be Bridget, would it?"

"Aye, it would be," he said back softly.

He gave me a look that told me of his emotions. A mixture of wonder and sorrow, and a fierce determination.

"We'll sort it out. We might just be nuts," he said.

"It's all relative," I said back. Because it was. What was "nuts"?

Einstein was nuts, but he was also the most brilliant man in recorded history. All of the greats like Edison, Jobs, Bezos, heck Howard Hughes. It's where we got the term "eccentric millionaire" from.

"Damn. You're an eccentric millionaire," I said.

"B," was all he said.

"Billionaire?" It couldn't be.

He winked at me. Well, hell, maybe it is love.

We had just parked at the pet store, and he swung out of the seat with a swagger I hadn't had the pleasure to see before. Smug bastard.

"You're lying."

"Would you like to see my bank account?"

"I mean, kind of, yeah."

He stopped mid-swagger to get his phone and pull up his bank app. Showing me the screen I had to count the commas to be sure. The number increased as I counted.

"Well, alright then."

"I've never seen someone so unenthused about billions of dollars."

"I mean, it just doesn't add up. Why are you with *me*?" I said again.

"Well, call me eccentric if you'd like. But I like being with you."

"Yes, but I don't understand why."

"You don't need to know why," he said as he kissed me before continuing to the store.

Billionaire, huh?

"What if this is your con?"

"Doesn't explain the house."

"Fair point."

"Then why am I driving all over?"

"You like control."

He wasn't wrong.

It's not that I didn't trust Declan. He knew that. It was the amount of times I'd been burned. And usually when something was too good to be true, it was.

Sid brushed into me briefly. Just a little touch to let me know he was there. I got the meaning. His awareness of my emotional state was keen.

Sid had lounged in the bushes while we were at the library. We didn't even tell him what to do. We'd hesitated, debating what to do with him, when he just went and laid behind a row of bushes in front of the plate-glass windows looking into the library.

Figuring he would stay we left him there. And he did, watching me all the while and following us to the car when we left.

Declan had gotten Sid out of the backseat as he was allowed in the pet store. We just had to put a collar and leash on him and then buy them. But for now he was ambling next to me, looking cheery in fact.

Declan set off ahead of me and I stared at his back in awe. All tall, broad shoulders and lean waist. Looking like he should be a bare-knuckle boxer, and yet he was brilliant. I was in so much trouble.

Walking in like he owned the place, Declan went for the collars and leashes and placed a chain link collar on Sid before clasping on the leash. Sid sat all the while, obediently allowing Declan to fasten him.

Maybe Sid's just a lost dog. He seemed like he had owners that cared for him before finding us. *But what about the seal creature?*

I had kind of forgotten about that. Hopefully, it was mentioned in one of the books I'd checked out.

As we walked the aisles, contemplating different purchases, I couldn't help but wonder if I hadn't misjudged Declan entirely. These new tidbits of information had me looking at him in a new light.

Had he always walked around like he owned the place? I was inclined to think that he did, and if memory served me, people tended to do his bidding.

Maybe that was why the table that first night we hung out was so monumental. Declan was used to people doing his bidding. He was probably aghast that someone had ignored his authority.

No, that wasn't quite right. I questioned authority like it was my job and he never bristled when I did. He was befuddled.

What was wrong with the table was that they had no acknowledgment of his authority. That fit more. Billionaires weren't used to being treated like a server. And servers rarely got the respect they deserved.

And of course, it explained the conversations. He was far smarter than the usual fare that worked in restaurants. I was an anomaly. Not to toot my own horn, but I took pride in my intelligence.

Why did I work in a restaurant? Because I lacked a true passion in life beyond reading books or helping people. And a psychology degree takes a lot of time. I would get one except I still hadn't managed to make enough money to do so yet.

So I served to get by. It was easy to work, I met a lot of cool people, and it was physically demanding. Every day was both the same as and different than the last and that was all right with me.

Though the real truth was that I had no self-esteem. So as smart as I thought I was, I still didn't think I was smart enough to amount to anything. And there have been plenty of people determined to dull my shine. So I stayed small hoping I went unnoticed.

Everyone has their skeletons.

What was Declan's? I found myself thinking about his past. Who was he when he wasn't with me? Who was he before me? So many things I guess I would discover in time.

We finished up at the store and it was already past 3 pm. There was maybe enough time to grab something to bring home to eat and still beat the traffic. Traffic was terrible everywhere in NJ. The worst times were 7-8 am, right now because school just let out, and between 5 and 7 pm. So our window was small if we were going to make it.

"Pizza?" Declan said.

"Yes," I said.

See? He already knew the key to my heart. I could eat pizza every day I think, a fact Declan was well aware of.

He called in our usual order while I drove to our place. In New York and New Jersey pizza places are on every other block, and which place was the best was a source of endless debate.

We liked the place by the mall—pepperoni, black olives, and onion on top of the pie, a chicken parm sandwich, and a chicken club. We split it all and had leftovers. I took a smaller portion of the sandwiches and the smaller slices.

It usually took five minutes to get there after work if we made it before they closed. Everything took five minutes at that hour, being so close to everything that needs getting to.

At this hour Route 1 was clogged with school buses, parents with their kids, and high school kids going who knows where. It took almost twenty minutes to go two lights, so the pizza was almost done by the time we got there.

"So are you going to elaborate on the billionaire status you just dropped on me before?" I asked him.

"I was waiting for that. I told you. I built and sold a few internet companies, not much to tell. My parents live in Ireland still. We come from a long line of well-to-do folk. Great-great-uncle years back was on the right side of things or so I understand. My brother and I started a consulting business after college. Sold that when it took off. People don't like to start their own businesses. It's tough going. So I started and sold a few more myself and here I am," he said with a shrug.

"Siblings?"

"Three brothers and one sister," he said.

That was also interesting information.

"Four sisters and one brother," I said back.

"Your parents are together?" I said, curiosity peaking.

"Yes since they were young. Twenty-five years together or so. What about yours?" he said.

"Nope, divorced when I was too young to remember. Both divorced from my stepparents too. So biologically I have one full-blood brother and four half-sisters divided between different parents," I said.

"You'll have to explain a bit," he said with a chuckle.

No surprise there.

"My mother had my oldest sister with her first husband when they were young and dumb and divorced. Because it was expected they marry, not everlasting love. She then met my father and had my brother and me. They divorced and each married my stepparents when I was around age seven. Then my mother had my sister with my stepdad, and my dad had two sisters with my stepmother. And now all parties are divorced again except my mother and stepdad are essentially still together. They just live separate and don't share bills if they can help it," I said as quickly and efficiently as I could.

"So that's what's wrong with you," he said with a wink.

He leaned over and kissed me, one bare hand covering my cheek and part of my neck. Leaning back with his hand still in place he looked into my eyes and stole my breath away.

"I'll keep you, Bridget," he said as he retook his seat.

Still staring at him, open-mouthed and dumbstruck, I wondered why he knew what I needed to hear. In two sentences and one gesture, he took a lot of fears off my plate.

*He doesn't know all of it yet. There's still plenty more to run him off with. Don't get your hopes up,* the stupid voice in my head chimed in.

"What's wrong with you then?" I said, teasing him.

"Don't worry your pretty little head. There's plenty wrong with me," he said as he reached over to squeeze my hand.

Our order was up so Declan got up to pay for it. I held the door for him as we made our way out, a liter of ginger ale in my hand.

It seemed silly that after all this time we didn't know intimate details about each other like that. I knew how he liked his coffee but not how many siblings he had. I knew my reasons for not talking about my family; I wondered what his were.

The ride home was spent mostly listening to music and enjoying the smell of pizza, taking in the scenery. New Jersey could be beautiful when it wanted to, and 287 north to 78 west heading into Pennsylvania was one of those routes.

As a kid, my brother and I used to go to my father's hunting club out this way where he'd hunt pheasant and deer. Sometimes we would go fishing on the river that's a part of the property. Those were good memories, mostly—the cold mornings in the mountains, where talking wasn't necessary.

We also went this way to my stepmother's family's house in Pennsylvania. It was on a lake and my favorite place to go as a kid. A lot of those memories stung now but I couldn't live in the past forever.

Lost in thought, I didn't notice Declan watching me.

"You can always talk to me you know," he said softly.

He had an uncanny ability to pick up on my thoughts. Somehow he always got the electric brain waves I was sending out into the universe. Every time he offered to listen. Always I declined.

"I'm all right, thanks," I said.

"You're more than all right," he said as he squeezed my thigh.

"I am now," I said as I grabbed his hand on my thigh.

Butterflies had erupted in my stomach at his touch. The promise of what this relationship might turn out to be was making me want to run for the hills or his bedroom. I wasn't entirely sure.

Well, maybe his bedroom first then I would run for the hills. That was more my style.

All I knew was that this was all happening both too fast and not fast enough with Declan. I had the overwhelming urge to jump in with both feet but also sabotage the whole thing. My usual reaction was to do something to ruin it if they didn't already.

My relationships to this point usually went one of two ways. In both cases, men ruined it by being exactly who I thought they were. How boring it was to dig deeper and find that they had no layers.

I tried dating nice guys who wouldn't hurt me. They never hurt me, they just bored me to death. It was like having sex with a priest, they were so fucking polite it made me want to puke.

And when I got bored the crazy leaked out in other ways, like binge drinking. Nice guys want to fix women with problems, treat me like the victim of my circumstances.

So they tried to help, and I got bored. Maybe I was a victim, but I wasn't helpless. And their endless patience with me was sweet really, thinking it would help me. It only helped me see how spineless they were.

No challenge, just meekly following me around like a puppy. It made me feel icky like I was using them, so I cut those ties quickly. I wanted a man not a puppy. I had enough spineless men in my life letting women push them around.

And then I would binge drink from boredom, self-sabotage, and that horrible feeling I got when I hurt them. They were only trying to help. And then I drank some more because I had to pull myself up by my bootstraps and keep moving because no one else was going to do it for me.

That was for damn sure.

Dating not-nice guys meant there were usually layers. But it still meant that they were who I thought they were, not nice.

Not-nice guys, their layers were childhood traumas that they never recovered from, and probably never would. That is why they're not-nice guys. They're content to live their lives without growing or changing. And they take their suppressed anger at their dad out on their girlfriends.

Then I was the victim all over again. Except then people said I asked for it, dating such a not-nice guy like him.

So then I drank to smother the pain while I welcomed some more in. Not-nice guys are good for forgetting your real problems because they make other problems for you. How thoughtful of them.

They're also good for supplying the alcohol to drown myself with. Then I would forget my problems lying on my back underneath them, just one more time. Because not-nice guys are not bad in bed. Maybe it's just the thrill of the pain they promise that gives it an edge of excitement.

The more digging I did with Declan, the more surprises I found, and the more I liked him. I didn't know much, but I knew I was definitely in trouble.

While I was pretty sure he was a nice guy, nice guys don't get ahead in life as Declan did. Nice guys find safe jobs that they toil their lives away at, never rocking the boat. They marry nice girls and have midlife crises after their kids are grown.

Successful businessmen weren't nice guys. They were cutthroat and ruthless and Declan had to have some of that considering his fortune and his age. There were still more mysteries surrounding him than answers. Either way I was already a goner.

He was definitely a nice enough guy but there was also that aura of danger surrounding him. That vibe that said he was nice by choice. He could be mean if necessary. A vibe I liked. Because I wasn't a "nice" girl.

I just hoped he really would keep me.

# CHAPTER 6

We got home, let Sid out and back in, and had just settled in to eat dinner in the living room when his phone rang.

"My mom," he said as he answered the phone.

Far past the stage of politeness, I dug into my food and tried to pay attention to the TV and not his conversation. He always finished his food faster than me anyway, even if I got a head start, so I was just saving us time.

Firmly trying to not pay attention, I couldn't ignore the tension in his voice when he said, "Dad?"

I tuned in then. From what I could tell it seemed as if his father had fallen ill, quite suddenly by the sound of it too.

So many questions came to mind. I didn't know his dad. Was he healthy? Did he have a history of health problems? I felt terrible, so I stopped eating, sat behind him, wrapped myself around him in as big a hug as I could.

He leaned back into me, one big hand wrapped around my ankle. I stopped listening again and just enjoyed the newfound intimacy in giving him comfort.

When he hung up, I scrambled around to face him, and he pulled me onto his lap. Burying his face in my hair, he squeezed me a few moments before pulling back.

"How would you like to go to Ireland with me?" he said softly. He didn't bother explaining, knowing I had listened in.

"Ireland?" I said breathlessly. It was a dream to go, but the circumstances weren't ideal.

"Well, I won't leave you here alone, with no one to watch your back, no offense to Sid. I know you'd love to go to Ireland and well, even if it's not ideal, I would love for you to meet my family."

"Are you sure?" I said. "I'd hate to impose. This is a delicate time for your family, hardly the time to meet new girlfriends. Or whatever," I mumbled the last part.

"That's just it, they won't just be meeting a new girlfriend, they'll be meeting *you*, Bridget. I have a hard time thinking of you as just a girlfriend."

He said the last staring into my eyes with an earnest look I had trouble denying. I was having trouble breathing.

"What would you call me then?" I whispered.

"Bridget, that's your name, isn't it?"

I smacked his shoulder.

"Oh, I don't know only I do know you're not just another girlfriend, and I don't think you're ready to be called more yet either."

He had a point.

"So you'll go then? I think it would be a welcome distraction for my mother, to fuss over you and not my father," he said.

"If you think so, but what about work?"

"I'll talk to Joe, and don't worry about the rest. I'll take care of you, Bridget. I promise," he said looking into my eyes. He must have seen the answer because he kissed me and called his mom again.

"We'll be there tomorrow," he said to her. After a few more minutes he said he loved her, and he hung up.

"You talk to your mom about me?" I said. He didn't explain who "we" was.

"Aye, you caught that, did you? Yes, I have. She's who insisted I protect you," he said chuckling.

"She did?" I said back.

"Aye. I called her when I saw you and the dog and told her I had a funny feeling. She's the one who told me about the cú sidh and explained their purpose. Real superstitious my mom is. She's why I've been successful, always telling me to follow my gut. When I told her I had a funny feeling, she told me to do whatever was necessary keep my eye on you and so I did." He said the last a little sheepishly.

It was a good look for him. I had never seen him so vulnerable.

"So she knows about us now?" Our relationship had changed from that first day.

"I have a mind to think she knew about us before we did. Can't say I've ever called home about a girl before you. Not that I haven't dated, just no one to call home about."

It was my turn to be a little sheepish and my damn Irish skin gave me away, blushing furiously.

He gave me a gentle kiss, quite a feat, smiling as broadly as he was. Shaking with laughter he moved me off his lap.

"I have a few more calls to make; Joe and arranging our trip. You eat, I'll only be a minute."

Nodding my approval, I knew I had a few phone calls to make. I may not have the best relationship with my parents, but I had to let them know if I was going that far away.

My father of course huffed and puffed, but he knew he couldn't tell me what to do so he conceded. My mother was jealous that she wasn't going with me, but she trusted me and with numerous, I love you's we hung up with my agreeing to keep her updated daily.

They both knew Declan already, so that wasn't a problem. They didn't know he was filthy rich, but I was always good with money. I just explained that his dad was sick, and I was there for support. I had just started back on the food when Declan came back in and sat down.

"All right, we leave first thing in the morning, 7 am. The flights about six hours and then it's a half hour to my home so we'll be there before dinner. Is there anything else you need from your place before then?" he asked, taking a bite of pizza.

"No, I think I'm fine, thanks."

"Well, if you think of anything I can send someone to get whatever you need. It's cold and wet. Do you have clothes for that?"

"It's cold and wet here. I think I'll be all right." My heart was racing actually, and I wasn't sure that I was all right. Going to Ireland? With Declan? To meet his family?

All the other nonsense flew out the window in light of this information. I wanted to go more than anything, but I was terrified to at the same time. What was I getting myself into?

One hand closed over the back of my neck, so he must have picked up on my spiraling thoughts. I gave him a weak smile. He pulled me closer to him and put on a show we liked to watch. It was funny, and we didn't have to pay full attention to it, but we always laughed.

Finishing half of the food we had ordered, he put the other half away while I took my bags upstairs to figure out what to bring with me to Ireland and what to leave here. I had gotten the bags upstairs and opened up before I really went mental. Packing was not my forte on my best day and today was not my best.

As I stared at the open bags in horror, Sid let out a low growl. I looked to see his haunches raised, tail low, and teeth bared, looking at something behind me. Afraid to look but knowing I had to, I braved a peek in the direction Sid was looking.

A man was standing in the corner of the room, glaring at me. How hadn't I seen him? He made an advance when I noticed him and Sid lunged, knocking him back into the wall.

The man looked startled like he hadn't seen Sid before the dog was on him. He had long dark hair and dark menacing eyes, clothed in all black.

He must have been in the corner, where it was heavily shadowed, the light of the moon from the skylight failing to penetrate the recess under the eave.

With one baleful look at me, he disappeared into thin air, leaving me dumbstruck. What the hell was *that*?

Unsure of what to do next, I just stood there a few minutes until Sid came up and licked me full on the cheek, breaking me out of my stupor. I rubbed him behind the ear and kissed him on the top of his head. What a good boy, protecting me. From what, I don't know, but it was Sid that scared him away, whoever he was.

Declan came crashing into the room. "What's wrong?" he said.

"How did you know something was wrong?" I questioned, weirded out.

"I don't know. I only knew I was putting the last of the food in the fridge when every hair on the back of my neck stood up. I came straightaway to find you and you look like you've seen a ghost."

I told him what happened as he was rubbing his hands on my arms to warm me up. I hadn't noticed the temperature in the room had dropped until he started. I was shivering head to toe.

"Come with me," he said when I finished.

He led the way back to the living room, and he went to the bookshelf to pull out a book. Finding the one he'd been searching for he opened it and rifled through pages until he found the right one.

"Carman" it said at the top. Glancing through it, Carman was described as being an evil Celtic witch, who with her three sons, spread trouble throughout Ireland before being driven across the sea by the Tuatha Dé Danann. Her three sons were Dub or "darkness," Dother or "evil," and Dain, "violence."

"So, what, you think that was darkness?" I said.

"I don't know but if I had to hazard a guess, this is what I came up with."

"But it says they were sent across the sea, defeated by the Tuatha Dé Danann."

"We're across the 'sea,' lass," he said.

"That's a bit of a stretch but maybe."

"Why now though?"

"I couldn't say but maybe a trip across the ocean would be good for a while."

"Why did you immediately know who it was?"

"Well, I told you I had been talking to my mom about you. And she's been researching this stuff since I brought it up. But the news about my dad, she thinks it was Carman that did it. And she has always been superstitious, so I really did grow up hearing stories like these."

"Do you have to tell me everything in increments?" I asked. It was like he told me one big thing at a time.

"My love, you're skittish on the best of days, and these haven't been the best of days."

Failing to find fault with his logic I agreed. Going to Ireland did seem like it could be a good idea. And I was definitely skittish. What didn't feel good was going back upstairs.

"I won't let anything happen to you, Bridget," Declan said softly.

"I know," I replied.

And I did know, but this was starting to feel more sinister. A few ravens and a cockroach, fine. Some seal creature, more weird than scary.

But the look on that man's face before he disappeared was pure hatred. It shone in the depths of his eyes and his body shook with pent up rage. I had never been the recipient of such hostility before and though I trusted Declan, he couldn't compete with a disappearing foe. I don't think. Maybe he would tell me that later.

Leading me back upstairs, Declan turned on every single light as he went. When we got to the bedroom, he went into the bathroom for a moment, returning with candles and a lighter. Setting them about the room, he lit each one until the corners that were obscured before were now bright.

"That ought to do it," he said.

"What? Light the house on fire?" I said, uncomfortable for the intimacy the candles lent the room.

He chuckled and closed the distance between us, grabbing my hips as he did so. He was not a nice guy, not when he grabbed me like that.

"You don't like my candles?" he said softly.

"It was very thoughtful of you," I said back.

It was. He always knew what to do to make me feel safe and comfortable, amongst other things. Like lust.

Leaning down, he kissed me gently. I felt it all the way to my toes.

"Finish packing," he said, and he smacked my butt.

Effectively breaking the tension, I smacked his butt too as I set off to do his bidding. Grateful for the escape he gave me, I went through my things about five times before I was satisfied I had everything I needed for the trip. He was done long before me and was lying on the bed, watching me with an amused expression.

"You going to pack until dawn?" he said with a grin.

I glared at him.

"Maybe."

"Come to bed. If you've forgotten anything we can buy it. Us Irish may be savages but we still have modern amenities."

Rolling my eyes, I got up and went to the bathroom first. I couldn't help myself I was panicking about lying in bed with him tonight. I wasn't at all tired enough to simply pass out when I got there, and I didn't trust myself being so close to him.

Clearly he wasn't my first boyfriend. I wasn't unfamiliar with how these things went, but this was already more serious than I wanted it to be. I didn't want serious.

Fun was fine. But I had my fill of fun already. Company was great, and you forgot about each other later. Fun was all I needed.

A serious relationship was next on the list, and Declan was a better candidate for serious than I thought I would have the pleasure to be with. It just felt so real all of a sudden.

I had tried relationships before and found them not to my liking. Nice guys never made it to relationship status. The only interesting guys were the not-nice kind, the liars, cheaters, and manipulators.

One in particular was incredibly nice to start with. Only to turn out to be the worst kind of person. You know, the ones that lie through their teeth while they smile and tell you they love you.

The ones that smile while they make you cry. The ones that get off on power trips and abusing women. That kind.

Declan wasn't that kind. I knew that much. But he wasn't a

"nice" guy either. That was the problem.

The problem was I did like Declan back like that. But I wanted to keep him as my friend. I didn't think having both was an option.

I had no positive relationship role models, so I had little faith they could work. And I had no positive relationships in my personal life to think I could make it work.

After spending too long in the bathroom I finally said fuck it. Or Declan, rather. Because I really did want to do that. Consequences be damned.

Exiting the bathroom, still feeling self-conscious, I made my way to the bed. Normally I'm confident in this area, it's not overly complicated. But I felt fit to burst with emotions I couldn't put my finger on.

"Would you relax?" Declan said when I got settled, a foot away from him on the bed.

"What are we doing, Declan?"

"Watching TV, you nut job. Now come here,"

Smiling, I moved closer and let him put his arm around me. Even as friends he'd put his arm around me, so it was a gesture I was fine with. Hell, even as friends it was a gesture I liked. There was a possessiveness about it that I liked, something primal like a caveman.

*Don't think like that!* My brain all but screamed at me too late.

"Now will you tell me what's the matter with you?" he said.

"You already know," I said back, slightly irritated, leaning up on my elbow to look at him.

He thought a moment before saying, "Aye, maybe I do. But I still think we ought to talk about it. Don't you women like to talk about things all the time?"

Damn.

"Sexist, since when was I a normal woman? What if it doesn't work out, Declan? I like having you as a friend."

"Pissing you off makes you talk. Maybe it won't. But you'll still have me as a friend; that doesn't have to change,"

"You know what I mean."

71

"Yeah, I do, but you know what I mean too. Bridget, we've been friends for over a year now. If we start this, the friendship doesn't disappear. We should be friends first, no matter what we add to the mix. I know who you are in here," he said as he put a finger above my heart, "and I know in here," he pointed to my head, "you wouldn't do anything to hurt me. That's all a relationship needs."

"That's not true. It needs a lot more, attraction for starters. And we haven't been friends that long. It's only been a few months,"

He started shaking with silent laughter.

"Bridget, I started there last summer. We've had two summers together now, don't you remember?"

"No! You're kidding!" I silently started going through memories. Damn it, he was right. Time does fly when you're having fun.

"And you're going to tell me there's no attraction between us," he said seductively.

"I didn't say that. I was making a point."

"Mmm, me too. Tell me, does the thought of this not working really scare you? Or is it the thought that it might?"

"Declan..."

"No really, is it that horrible to think of spending your life with me?"

He knew the answer to that. He was just being difficult.

"Life?"

He rolled his eyes.

"Then what, Bridget?" he said.

"Then what, I don't know 'then what,' Declan. What if you find out you don't like me all that much? Maybe I'm boring or I'm too whiney or I chew too loud," I said.

"You do whine too much," he said.

He got a whack to the chest for that one.

"Quit your complaining. If I found you boring, I probably would have stopped hanging out with you months ago. You don't chew too loud, and I like that you have a hearty appetite. And your whining is justified, at least most of the time," he said.

"Hearty appetite, huh?"

"You eat near as much as me and you're a quarter of my size. I never know where you put it until you give me a smack because of a smartass remark I make and then I remember it's all in these muscles."

He gave my bicep a squeeze. I was teased incessantly growing up for my muscles but there wasn't anything I could do about them. They insisted. I've since outgrown the insecurity around them in favor of knowing I could protect myself. I didn't need a man for that job.

"Do you good to keep them in mind before you make more stupid remarks," I said.

"I like your muscles. And I like your fire. Bridget, there's little about you I don't like."

"What don't you like?" I said.

"Walked into that one, didn't I?"

"I'd say so."

"I don't like your scars, love. I don't like knowing someone could hurt you with no remorse. I like who your scars made you, but if I had my choice, I'd make everyone pay for what they did to you," he said softly.

I'm in so much trouble.

"Did I pass?" he said.

"This round," I joked.

"Keep it coming, Bridget. Give me all you got," he said as he kissed me lightly.

Gently rolling me onto my back and leaning over me, he deepened the kiss. Fire erupted deep in my belly, and it wasn't just lust. It was hope.

# CHAPTER 7

I woke up in the early morning light aching in all the best places. A night with Declan was exactly what I thought it would be. Every bit satisfying, addictive, and intense.

Life always felt like I couldn't get any satisfaction. There was always a hole in my chest where satisfaction should have been. Last night changed that. He had filled me completely, in more than one sense.

I was more than content right now.

This wasn't a gentle romance we had. It was all-consuming. There was a desperation to it like we couldn't bear to have any space between us. Physically and metaphorically tearing down the walls between us. I liked it. A lot.

He must have too because once he turned the alarm off he turned to me, and we spent another half hour tangled together. I think I could get used to this.

I'd been nervous last night, not just because of it being our first time together but also because, what if it sucked? And what if the spark was short-lived?

I don't think I've ever been more wrong. While I can't say that the spark will last forever, I can say the sex was incredible. Like all-consuming, mind-blowing, toe-curling sex and I wouldn't mind if the honeymoon phase lasted forever.

And now I can say that if we didn't last together forever it would be okay because at least I'd had sex like that. It was explosive and passionate and everything I was looking for but had never found. Some of my fears abated but others popped up. Except right now I couldn't give less of a fuck.

After he made coffee, we showered together and wasted a little bit of time in there too. Finally, we were satisfied enough to get moving, far too late.

"What?" he said.

"I don't want to miss the plane!" I said anxiously as he drove. He just laughed.

Now it was my turn to say, "What?"

"They won't leave without us, Bridget. It's my plane,"

"Ugh, of course it's your plane,"

"You have a problem with me having my own plane?"

"No, it's just that you're too perfect."

"Don't worry, I'm not perfect."

"You seem way too good to be true," I said truthfully.

"I can ruin that soon enough. You're going to meet my family, remember?"

"You got nothing on my family."

"I didn't know we were competing."

"Either way, you're winning at life and I'm not."

"I think you're winning. After all, you're dating me," he said with a laugh.

I whacked his thigh. Smart ass.

"You know, most women are impressed by me. Well, my money at least," he said.

"I'm not most women," I said back.

"True enough," he said with a squeeze of my hand.

It was still early, the sun was just lightening the sky, and I was fully enjoying watching the sleeping world go by in Declan's car. He chose his Jeep to drive today. Not overly expensive as cars went but the winter weather was more suited to the Jeep.

He also had a Challenger, but that wasn't good for winter in New Jersey. Declan and I shared a love of American muscle cars so I got in that thing as much as I could.

Feeling the full effects of last night, I was pretty melted into the seat, and I let myself drift off. Declan woke me when we got to the airport.

It was one of those one-lane, private airports. We hadn't

driven long, and I recognized the area. A small jet was waiting for us on the runway, a pilot standing at the top of the stairs. Declan parked in the hangar, and we made our way to the plane, Sid in tow.

I was glad for my exhaustion. Not having much experience flying I was slightly terrified. The last time I did I was a kid going to Florida, but I barely remember it.

We made our way onto the plane, the pilot taking my bags for me, and I was shocked by the luxury. I shouldn't have been, but Declan had a way of surprising me by not flaunting his wealth like a lot of people can.

I knew a man at one of the restaurants I had worked at that bought a new Porsche every year in a custom color he liked, a powder blue. He only wore four-hundred-dollar shirts, his teeth were blindingly white to match his too-white hair, and his skin was super tan.

We knew when he would be in so we put his wine on ice, white Zinfandel, and we would save the bottle for him for the next day if he didn't finish it. He was a nice guy, actually, but he liked to show off his money. I don't blame him, either. I might too if I was filthy rich.

Declan wasn't like that. Even now he was dressed in black boots, jeans, a thermal, and a thin jacket. For all, I knew it cost a couple thousand, but it wasn't flashy. The jeans fit him particularly well and I wasn't so tired anymore.

He introduced me to the pilot, Patrick, and they seemed to know each other well. An older man, Patrick wore his age well, with laugh lines surrounding his eyes that danced when he shook my hand. He was tall and lanky, with graying hair under his hat.

"Bridget, it's a pleasure to meet you," he said, his voice a deep timbre, heavily accented with a brogue.

"You too," I said and meant it. He looked the sort of person I could get along with.

Another man made his way out of the cockpit, younger with sandy hair cut short and bright blue eyes, tall and lean too but with more muscle than Patrick. He was introduced as Eric, the copilot, and he would be responsible if we needed anything.

Smiling and shaking his hand I wondered what else we could need. Would I order him to get the bottle of water just beyond my reach? I laughed to myself at the idea, but I knew plenty of people that would do it. Heck, my one sister did it with my mom and we weren't rich, nor was she incapable of getting it herself.

Sid was already lying comfortably on the floor, but I worried about what he would do when we took off. Declan set those fears aside when he told me that he had a crate for Sid tucked away in the back of the plane, where there was a bed.

He asked if I would be more comfortable in the back, but I thought I'd rather be with him. I was small enough to sleep in one of the seats if I wanted to and I could always keep Sid company if necessary.

I feared he would fare better without company though, not being used to being crated. Like how babies don't mind being in cribs if they wake up and are playing alone, it's when they see mom or dad they get upset.

All settled, we buckled up and put on the big TV in the front, though I had brought books to read to keep me occupied. He put on a movie I loved though so I had a hard time paying attention to the book. There wasn't a peep from Sid as we took off, so I squelched the urge to check on him.

I fared better than I thought I would, and we were up in the air cruising comfortably when I realized it. He tricked me into it by putting on a movie I liked and letting me meet the pilots. Realizing this I glanced his way to see the smirk on his face.

"Caught me, did you?" he said smiling.

God but that smile. "Good work, I barely paid attention."

"That was the idea," he said, unbuckling and coming over to kiss me.

That kiss lasted a while longer than I think either of us intended, and by the end of it, I was unbuckled and straddling his lap.

"More distractions?" I said when I came up for air.

"You find me distracting?" he said his eyes sparkling with mischief.

That was a favorite look of mine I decided.

He pressed a button and said, "We're all alone now."

"Here?" I said, slightly embarrassed.

"They won't bother us unless I buzz them in, and now they won't because I've told them not to."

"Ugh, but now they know!" I whisper shouted.

"They don't know anything. Besides, like they couldn't figure it out for themselves,"

"Well, what we do elsewhere is our business. I'd be mortified if they came out here!"

"They won't," he said as he kissed me again.

I could feel my arguments leaving me as he deepened the kiss and ran a hand under my shirt. He fought dirty.

✳ ✳ ✳

Sated and dressed again, he sat on the bench seat, legs on the seat in front of us as I curled up on my side, laying with my head on his thigh.

"You're trouble, you know that right?" I said looking up at him.

"I could say the same about you."

He gently ran his hand through my hair, flowing over his lap.

"You wouldn't want me any other way," he said quoting a song we liked.

"You may be right," I said back, both naming the song and answering him.

The song was "You may be right," by Billy Joel. It was a song that the piano man played Friday nights at work, very loudly I might add.

Declan and I joined in when he played it, in between taking care of tables. There were a few songs we sang together like that. We had a lot of fun together. Which made me think...

"Declan, what do you do with the money from work?" I asked.

"Donate it. I put it into a separate account and when it hits a certain amount, I send it to different foundations," he said back.

"What kind of foundations?"

"Depends, sometimes just to different food banks or homeless shelters, other times to endangered animals. I give Joe a portion too. I like to make as much impact as I can."

"He knows? No wonder he loves you so much. You did all of this to get close to me?"

"If it's easy, it won't be worth it. If it's worth it, it won't be easy," he quoted.

"Hmmm, worth it, huh?"

"Too early to tell," he joked.

I just smiled to myself. Worth it. I suppose he was too.

✽ ✽ ✽

I must have drifted off because he was shaking me awake and I was disoriented.

"Sleepyhead, get up," he said as I stirred.

"Are we there already?"

"Soon. I knew you'd want to see the countryside from the plane, and you can just see land off in the distance."

I gave him a kiss for his thoughtfulness. Sitting up and rushing to the window I peered out, and everything was green and blue as far as I could see.

"It's beautiful, Declan. Thank you," I said earnestly. Then a thought crossed my mind. "I never did ask you where we were going did I?"

I knew he was from near Galway, Declan O'Connor. My grandfather fancied himself our family historian, so I knew I was from Cork originally, Bridget O'Connell. Wheels started turning in my head.

"O'Connor near Galway. Surely not descended from the king O'Connor?" I said.

"And what do you know about Irish kings, O'Connell?"

"Not much. I know that he was supposed to be the last high king, uniting Ireland."

"Yes, that'd be the one."

"So you're like royalty?"

"If you say so. I wouldn't. But in a nutshell, I'm like royalty. I told you an uncle aligned himself well. Our original surname may not have been O'Connor, but we know from that uncle that he was one."

"Great you just keep getting better," I said sarcastically.

"You could be enthused about it. Most women would love to date royalty. Why not you?"

"Well, I hardly packed for meeting royalty for starters, and second I think I'd like to brush up on my manners before meeting them."

"Your manners are impeccable, and your clothes are fine. We're not true royalty. You're not going to meet the queen."

"Still, it adds a lot of pressure to the whole thing."

"If you say so."

"Where do you live anyway?"

"The name is Ennis. It's near Galway but about an hour away," he said.

"Do you live in a mansion?" I said, suddenly horrified at the idea.

"You'll have to see for yourself, won't you?"

"That's evasive."

"Just enjoy the view and quit your worrying."

I did just that and he wrapped an arm around me, pulling me closer. You would think I'd be excited but truthfully I felt dread. Dread and self-deprecation. I'm not worthy of all of this. This happens to richer, skinnier, prettier women—not me.

Trying to abate the depression that would surely follow that particular line of thought I focused really hard on the view in front of me. This really was all surreal...

"There has to be something wrong with you," I said suddenly.

"Bridget, hush," he said gently.

Yeah, all right. In one sense he had never lied to me outright, in the other he lied by omission. It was all too good to be true. One way or the other I was in too deep now to back out so I may as well continue on this path and see where it led.

The view was stunning, green everywhere interspersed with lakes and other bodies of water. I caught a few glimpses of castles and churches. I couldn't wait to explore a few.

And a few graveyards! I know how morbid it is, but I love to imagine a person's life that came and went thousands of years ago.

In the excitement, I could almost forget what really brought us here. Declan put on a good show, but he was anxious. Taking care of me helped, so I tried to keep him focused on me but as we drew nearer his mood became blacker.

Holding his hand I asked, "Would you like to talk about it?"

"No," he said with a small smile.

"Well, how about you tell me what I'm getting myself into? I deserve a warning."

"We have the car ride for that," he said as he kissed me with urgency.

Who was I to deny him?

\* \* \*

People deal with things in all different ways. Declan was a fan of ignoring the issue until you had to face it. It was my preferred method too.

I prepared myself but I also liked to avoid as much unnecessary worrying as possible. Some people called me cold, but I think it's more a logical thing. There's quite literally nothing to gain from worrying for worrying's sake.

After we bid farewell to the pilots, me trying to avoid eye contact as much as I could by taking in the scenery, we collected Sid and hopped into a Range Rover.

"Where to first?"

"We'll get settled before we visit. We could freshen up first," he smirked.

"Good idea, where are we visiting?" I asked. He still hadn't told me anything, and I hated to pry but I needed to know.

"They're at home. My mum worries over much and my dad is stubborn.

"The long and short of it is my father was a drunk for many years when I was young. My mother was sick during those years after my sister's birth, and she was in the hospital, so she didn't know.

"He has complications from those years of not taking care of himself. He's fallen ill in the past but he's not getting any younger. The compromise is nurses at home.

"This time he seems to have gotten sick quickly and they aren't sure what happened yet. That's what I'll help sort out."

"How?"

"Any way that I can. Something seems fishy or else my mom wouldn't have called me in. He's only gotten sick recently,"

"They must love each other."

"That they do. My father hasn't had a drop of alcohol since my mom had him quit."

"Do you think that's what happened?"

"The thought crossed my mind."

"Declan is that why you never drink?"

"That doubled with my inability to drink successfully. What about you?"

So he had caught that.

"My mom, and it became the only thing I ever felt like doing," I said softly.

"Yes, drowning your sorrows sounds nice but you only add to them don't you?"

"Yeah, well, it was fine in theory, but I've never heard of someone successfully drowning their worries."

"No, I don't suppose I have either. I don't regret it. I learned a few lessons the hard way but if I hadn't I reckon I never would have learned them," he said.

"Yeah, I can agree with that. Some lessons I could have done without, but in reality, I'm not the docile type. The only way I learn is the hard way more often than not."

"Ha, now that's a truer statement than any I've heard out of your mouth."

"Pot calling the kettle black."

"I already told you, Bridget, your fire is what I love about you. A lot of people live their lives always playing it safe, too afraid of what is outside of the little box they created for themselves. You live outside the box."

"Takes one to know one."

"True enough," he said as he reached over to grab my hand.

People always tried to put me in a box. It was a source of anger and anxiety for me. Try as I might, I could never mold myself to their expectations of me.

Which in turn made me feel that there was something inherently wrong with me or angry that they thought there was. In time I learned to embrace it, but it still chafed.

"Tell me more about your family," I said after a few minutes.

"My parents have been together forever. They both come from wealthy families and though it was a favorable match, it was one borne of love. I know my father drank in his younger years as any good Irishman would but when they got married and had me he had put it down to be a family man."

"So you're the oldest?"

"Yes, then came my two younger brothers, Rory being the oldest and closest in age to me. He's two years younger. Siobhan is the youngest and only girl."

"Which makes him..." I interrupted.

"Huh, you don't know how old I am, do you? He's twenty-eight, making me thirty and you twenty-four."

"Yes but I don't remember telling you that."

"No, you didn't. Shortly after I started working with you I noticed some things that were slipping under Joe's radar and so I brought a few things up to him and he asked me to take a closer look. Taking a closer look meant I had access to your basic information when it came to payroll, like your date of birth."

"That would further explain your relationship with Joe. I thought it was just that Joe fancied us together, and that's why he had some hero worship of you going on."

"Hero worship, huh? Do you worship me too?"

"Don't flatter yourself."

"Too late. Yes, when I got there Joe had little to no inventory management and he was leaving a lot of money on the table. I just helped him nail down his numbers, put a few systems in place, and maximize his profits and losses."

"That was very kind of you."

"Joe's a good man, and in truth, he would have been all right, but hopefully now he'll be better than all right. He did fancy us together though,"

"That's no surprise. It's probably also why he was so agreeable to us taking off work together."

"He sounded quite proud of himself."

"So tell me more."

"More, fine, well my youngest and only sister came last. She was not exactly expected and is younger than me by fifteen years."

"So she's fifteen now?"

"Yes, and she's a pip. Not unlike yourself."

"We should get along fine then," I joked.

"That you should. As I said, my mother was older then, and she had several complications during and after the pregnancy which led to multiple surgeries and a few years of bed rest. She's fine now, thank God. This all was happening when my father's company had been expanding and hit numerous roadblocks. Granted, we had wealth already, but this was my father's life's work. He took it seriously and the combination of the responsibilities took its toll on him."

"Understandable."

"Yes, now—during the time, not as much. At the time I was a young and dumb kid who had a dream life that came crashing down. The more my father spent away from us, at work and the bar, the more I took up the helm at home and the more resentment I built."

"It's a tough age any way you slice it."

"It is, and while we had cooks, nannies, and the like, we didn't have our parents. People seem to think money solves all problems, but we still had our issues before this, and those problems grew as a result. I was always a difficult child for instance."

"Shocking."

"My younger brother was thirteen at the time and as kids that age do, he had his own life already and didn't have time for us. Not to say I blame him, but I didn't understand then either."

"You always think you do, but you don't. Ok Rory, Declan, Siobhan…"

"Brian and Patrick."

"O'Connor."

"We're Irish."

"Could've fooled me."

"Your turn, *Bridget*," he said with emphasis. I was very Irish too.

I started where I always start. "My mom had my oldest sister, Jane, when she was young. They got married because that's what you did then and that didn't work out. She's nine years my senior. Then my mother met my father a few years later and had my brother Michael, who is two years older, and then me.

"That lasted longer, about seven years but I was only two when they split. Both stepparents were in the picture when I was four or so. I remember kindergarten with them in it. I was eight when Alice was born and twelve and fourteen for Mary and Ann. Mom and stepdad split at the end of high school and dad and stepmom at the end of college."

"Do you have a chart?"

"Ha."

"So your mom…"

"It's not easy marrying three of the wrong men I imagine. If not wrong, all couldn't handle the responsibilities at the time. Her first marriage, they were too young. My dad thought himself an adult and a hero but he's still a bit of a spoiled brat. Same for my stepdad without the hero part.

"She leaned on me for my one younger sister because my oldest sister was already out of the house, my brother had gotten older and had his own life, and my stepdad was in his own world. Life wasn't fair to my mom and her choices weighed on her in the worst way."

"Keen insight."

"Well, takes one to know one. In my anger at the world, I became a lot like her. Life wasn't fair to her, or me in many ways, but I had the benefit of seeing what it does to people, anger."

"Festers."

"You know a thing or two about anger?"

"A thing or two, that was the other side of the story. The more lost in the bottle my dad became the angrier he became too. Not violent towards us kids, just angry, walking on eggshells around him. I got angry when I drank too but the violent kind. Many men feel the need to prove their mettle at that age, but it wasn't a way to be."

"Many men aren't as big as you though."

"Therein lied one problem. The other problem was if they were as big as me."

"Got in a lot of fights?"

"Not too much but enough—enough to know that I needed to stop."

"Did you go to a program?"

"Yes. I had to get my head straight. Only I didn't know they would help with all of the other issues too,"

"That's what I hear. My best friend Jared had gone and has told me a lot about it. I haven't but I've seen therapists before."

"And you're still allowed to be with the general population?"

"That was a good one."

"I thought so myself."

I enjoyed being able to laugh at our issues. Laugh at ourselves. If you can't laugh at yourself, you can't laugh at anyone else.

"Then what?" I asked.

"Then I built my fortune with Rory. We had started it before I became a complete ass, and I worked all the while I was a mess but the best that came of it was afterward. I developed a healthy lifestyle and routine. And I built and sold a few more companies."

"And you're Ireland's most eligible bachelor?"

"Seems I'm a bachelor no more."

"You know what I mean."

"Yes, I dated other women. Few for long."

"Many women?"

"Do you really want to know?"

"I mean that's already an answer."

"Yes, Bridget, more than a few, but even the ones I dated publicly I never called my mom about."

"Hmmm." That placated me for now.

"And what about yourself, miss? Pester me, it's your turn."

"Hmmm...More than a few," I said back staring at the floor.

"I'll still keep you, Bridget," he said softly as he squeezed my hand. He could tell it was a button he'd pressed.

Truthfully I shouldn't have asked if I didn't want to answer the question myself, but I couldn't quite harp on why he would shackle himself with me. Of all women why me? I was the definition of damaged and he was *everything.*

"Bridget?" he said tentatively.

"Yes?"

"Why can't you just accept that I want you?"

"Loaded question."

"Valid question. You're smart, strong, beautiful, witty, kind, and all of those lovely things. I hate seeing the ghosts in your eyes, Bridget."

"More for another day. Besides, you can't blame me when you blindsided me with your true identity."

"My identity aside, you never wanted to let me close."

"Do you harangue all of your girlfriends this early on?"

"I'm asking my best friend who always kept me at arm's length."

"Harder to hurt me that way."

"Keep hurting yourself that way. I can help bear the burdens if you let me."

"Why would you want to?"

"Bridget, you're going to make me say it aren't you?"

"Say what, Declan?"

"That I love you, you stubborn idiot."

That got me to shut up for a minute.

"Stubborn idiot?"

"You're going to focus on that?"

"Fine. I love you too. Even if you're an ass."

"That's better, now you could act like you like the fact that we love each other and not like a child who didn't get her way."

"Well I already knew you loved me, but it could have been said more romantically."

"I love you, Bridget," he said with emphasis. "How was that?"

I smacked his thigh again.

"Significantly worse," I said back.

But I was smiling ear to ear, and that was his goal after all.

"You do love me, don't you?" I said after a while.

"If it's all right with you I'd like to for a long time."

"What's a long time, a month?"

"We can start with that," he said, grabbing my hand and kissing my knuckles.

We can start with that.

* * *

Pulling off the main road and onto the private drive to his home, we were met with wrought-iron gates and a box next to the car that Declan entered a passcode into to open them. Past the gates was a long drive and green grass and trees as far as the eye could see but no house yet. It was giving me a bad feeling. Sid could still care less, asleep on the backseat.

"Declan, just how big is this house?" I asked.

He had a wicked grin that split his face.

"Before you go getting ahead of yourself it's a family home, not one I bought myself."

I groaned. I was going to feel so out of place among all of this luxury.

"Don't be so excited," he said wryly.

"I just feel like I'll stick out like a sore thumb."

"Would you like me to buy you a wardrobe to match the luxury?"

"No! I don't want you wasting money on me!"

"I have more than enough to waste."

"But then I'd feel like a gold digger."

"Bridget I have to fight with you to let me date you; you're the furthest from a gold digger."

He had rounded a bend in the drive and the house came into view. If you could call it a house.

It was all white, done in Georgian style, with a black roof. It was an old home. I couldn't put my finger on the date but at a minimum in the 1800s, it had been built.

To the right was a small glen and beyond that a small lake. It was positioned on the top of a hill overlooking both. All long square windows allowing for a great view. Directly above the front door was a little patio. I wondered if you could walk out there to see the water.

Driving past the house he pulled around to the left and in the back was what must have been stables and servant quarters. These were gray brick with red brick around the doors and windows, giving them a quaint look. They were connected to the main home in a Z shape, the carriage houses connecting the main home to the servant's homes.

Declan parked in an alcove that was once for horses and carriages but now served as a carport for the same purposes. All of us getting out, I was having a hard time being anything but in awe at the property. Thinking of the dozens of lives that had come and gone here had me reverent as I ran my hand along the stones that made up the walls.

"I thought you'd like it here. No one ever uses this property, instead staying with our parents when we're here. But I thought you'd prefer the space here and the history," he said.

"Declan, it's amazing, thank you." I was still a little awestruck.

"Come inside, the view is even better from there. I had our people come out and freshen up, stock everything, and wash the linens. We still maintain the property and we rent it out for special occasions but rarely use it for ourselves."

He led the way as I soaked up everything I could. Grabbing my hand to keep me from tripping, he chuckled.

"I thought you weren't a gold digger. You seem fine with it all now."

"This is about the history. Declan, when was this built?"

"Right around your country's independence, 1770s."

Following Declan to the front door, I glanced over the water to the trees beyond. It was a sight to see, the countryside sprawling out in front of me, a sight I'd never tired of.

Swiveling my head back to Declan, something moved in the shadows of the trees. Whipping my head back I didn't see anything, but goosebumps had erupted over my skin.

"Bridget?" Declan was standing stock still staring in the direction I just was.

"Did you see anything?"

"I'm not sure but I don't think we're alone either."

Staring another few minutes at the tree line without seeing anything else we continued on ahead.

"Wait, where's Sid?" I asked.

"He took off when we got out of the car while you were busy drooling."

"I wasn't drooling. Maybe that was Sid over there," I said, more to ease my fears than anything.

"Could be. It's narrow across the water there. Maybe he wanted a swim,"

Shrugging we both went inside. Sid was a dog kind of, but we both treated him like he was his own man. And he was, we had no rights to him, so we trusted him with the same level of trust he lent us. If he came back, great. If not, he wasn't ours to keep anyway, and he didn't seem to need us. I'm sure he'd be back though.

Inside the front door was a large staircase dominating the foyer, leading up to a landing that split into two different hallways. At the top of the stairs directly in front of us was a large plate-glass window decorated with different sets of coats of arms, with green as a background, bordered by blue.

In the foyer, there were only the stairs to be seen, with four doors leading to different rooms. The banister to the staircase was ornately carved wood, dark wood for the handrail, posts, and stairs. The inside of the banister was delicately done with carving in white, so much detail it reminded me of lace. The parquet floors were a lighter wood done in a chevron pattern.

Exploring different rooms the pattern remained, with white crown molding throughout in a beautiful pattern, the same pattern surrounding the windows. Upstairs the molding surrounded patio doors that did lead out to the little deck overlooking the lake.

This room was huge, with two built-in bookshelves fully stocked lining the wall opposite the windows and doors. A giant fireplace stood immediately in between. The ceiling was equally intricately carved with a circular pattern of the white molding that dominated the rooms.

All bedrooms were neat and tidy with period furniture decorating the space. The bathroom had a claw-foot tub that looked inviting. I imagined myself with a book from the library, soaking in the tub.

Back downstairs in the living room, there was a large cathedral-style window overlooking the property. Everything was bright and shiny and well maintained, with numerous updates having been done to preserve the integrity of the property. It would be a lovely place to get married or vacation in and I understood why they kept the property and rented it out.

"Satisfied?" Declan asked. He'd quietly followed me in my exploration, amusement apparent on his face all the while.

"For now," I said. There was so much more to explore, like the stables, the kitchen, the property itself. But we had more important things to do today.

"Aye, for now. We're expected at my parents in another hour, so we have about a half-hour to freshen up. Come with me, I have something for you."

Curiosity peaking I followed without argument. Following him back up the stairs he reached out to grab my hand again, anticipation coiling low in my belly. I couldn't seem to get enough of his touch.

And this was why I was afraid of starting this with him. I was in too deep before we'd even slept together. Now that we had, I was vulnerable. Walls had been torn down that could never be put back up again.

He led me into the master bedroom, denoted by the size of the room and the view outside of the window. Letting go of my hand and opening a closet door filled with clothes he pulled out one emerald dress and laid it on the bed. It wasn't overly formal, with long lacy sleeves, a tight bodice covered in the same lace, and a long flowing skirt, it looked warm enough for the weather while maintaining its beauty.

"I thought this would be a good first impression for my parents. Seeing as I knew you would feel like you needed to buy a new wardrobe, I had someone do just that," Declan said softly.

"It's beautiful, Declan, thank you." I didn't have shoes for it though. Or a coat. But I didn't want to take away from the gesture by saying so.

"And if you look in the closet, you'll see the accessories were taken care of as well."

Well, how about that?

"You went through all this trouble for me?"

"It's no trouble and besides, I wanted to see you wear this dress like you couldn't believe. So it's a selfish move on my part." He winked at me.

Oh, man. I'm in so much trouble.

"How did you know what size to get?"

"Your dirty laundry at my house. After we left I had my assistant clean them and get your measurements and I had an assistant here buy the clothes."

"Sounds like something serial killers do."

"You're welcome," he said back, and I laughed.

"Thank you. Honestly this is the most thoughtful thing anyone's ever done for me," I said as I kissed him.

Looking at the dress I couldn't help the selfish thought that I didn't have beautiful undergarments to accompany such a beautiful dress. Biting my lip I ran my hand over the material.

"Top drawer over there," Declan said.

Walking over to open the dresser drawer I saw lots of lacy garments to go under the dress. Desire flooded me just thinking of wearing all of this around Declan. Damn it he is so much trouble.

Coming up behind me, Declan settled a hand on my hip and the other over my belly. My breath left me in a rush and my heartbeat was in my throat.

"You'll look lovely, Bridget,"

"Isn't this all a bit much?"

"No, my father is lucid, only weak. He's on painkillers and bedridden but they can't determine what the cause is. In truth, my mother thinks his illness is connected to you and she thought us all together would best solve the mystery.

"We will be having dinner with my family tonight. It's not a formal affair, but I thought this would be comfortable as well as beautiful. Oh, and it has pockets, and it will go with these riding boot looking things, so it dresses it down."

"You thought of everything, didn't you?"

"I tried. In truth my assistants thought of everything. Lovely ladies, and I pay them well to think of it all."

"Well, I appreciate it. Tell them thank you for me."

"I will. I'm glad you're happy," he said as he kissed me lightly.

"You have a lot of ladies working for you? By the way, you seem to keep trying to rationalize everything that's going on, but your mother is the one urging you to accept it's all supernatural," I said after a minute.

"She's a good Irishwoman. She has all the old wives' tales memorized, and she believes in leprechauns. I grew up thinking her eccentric, but logic doesn't exactly explain what's been happening lately. And, no, the only ladies in my personal detail employment are the housekeepers. Also, no it's not a sexist thing, I only had lady applicants."

"Likely story. Are they pretty ladies? And you didn't tell me specifics with your dad because your mom has outlandish hypotheses for what's been going on."

"Something to do with us being fated to vanquish Ireland's evildoers. The veil to the other realm being open again. Things of that sort. They are lovely older ladies that I find in no way attractive to me personally."

"Us?" I let the cleaning ladies slide finally. I'd just wanted to hear it from his lips.

"Yes, us. I had called her bonkers a few times but I'm not certain anymore. Seeing as I can't keep my hands off of you I'm beginning to believe in a strong connection here."

"Lust doesn't qualify as a strong connection," I said.

"You feel it too. It's more than that."

"Maybe, but you really thought of all the things *that* would be what scared me away?"

"Well, Bridget you've been skittish since the day I met you. I only give you what I think won't send you packing."

"Probably the right call," I said.

"Definitely the right call," he said with a laugh. "Now get dressed and let's go,"

He kissed me on the cheek and let me go to get dressed. Stripping off his shirt I had time to ogle a bit. Lean muscles covered every inch of him, piled high from use. His pants were next, and I couldn't tear my eyes away.

"You're drooling again," he said.

My hand flew to my lip. I was not. But I was overtly staring. Undressing myself it was his turn to watch, and I gave him a show.

"No time now, but later," he said with a growl that made my insides clench.

# CHAPTER 8

We made it to his parents' house on time and it was no less lavish than his two properties we had visited, only more modern. Sid had not shown up yet, so we left without him but left a carriage door open for him if he wanted to get warm. Declan told me the housekeepers would be there soon anyway so not to worry about Sid as he prepped me on the way to his parents.

His mother was exceedingly warm and would fuss over me with his sister in tow. Though affectionate she was no less introverted than me, so we would get along.

Siobhan was more outgoing and had his father's tendency to blurt things, like me. His father was a harder man, loved his family fiercely, but he didn't strike anyone as warm.

Rory, his brother closest in age, shared their father's likeness and demeanor. Patrick and Brian were rambunctious and wild and with Siobhan they all got into mischief with his mother's aid often. All were straightforward and would ask inappropriate questions. Sounding like my own family I figured I would be alright.

Holding my hand as he opened the door his mom was the first to rush to us. Hugging and kissing Declan first she turned her attention on me, and I got one of the warmest hugs I had ever received.

"Bridget! Finally, I get to meet you! I wish the circumstances were more pleasant dear, but I thank God you found my boy," she said.

"It's a pleasure to meet you, Mrs. O'Connor," I said.

She seemed awful happy with me already. She might be the

first mom to say that to me I thought wryly.

"Joan dear, call me Joan. Come, let's eat. It's all ready for you. The two of you must be starving,"

I gave Declan a look as we followed his mom. He was laughing. At me or his mother, I didn't know.

"I hope your travels were well," his mom said.

"Yes, fine Mom. Better now," Declan answered.

Pulling out my seat for me at a long, dark wood table that was filled with food, Declan introduced me to everyone. His father was in a wheelchair at the head of the table and though his pallor was sickly, his eyes were sharp.

He was a big man, like Declan, but his hair and eyes were dark, and his pale skin had the redness drinkers often get. Gin blossoms were evident on his nose but not obnoxiously.

Rory, Brian, and Siobhan shared his coloring while Declan and Patrick favored their mother. Joan was a spry little thing, slight but solid with red hair dulled by age but her green eyes were still bright, the shade of emeralds.

Both sons had hair and eyes not as vibrant as their mother but lovely all the same. Siobhan was slightly taller and bigger than her mother, but both were similar in height to my own.

"Where's the cú sidh?" his mother said.

"It's a dog, Joan," his father, Brian Sr. said.

His mother *tskd* at him and turned her attention back to Declan.

"Out," was all he replied.

"Oh, good. We're in no danger tonight then. Best you let him free to roam. Now eat," she said.

Passing around pot roast, mashed potatoes, carrots, and other accompaniments I felt very at home as they took up conversations among themselves. Not feeling left out, I dug in as I listened along. I noticed Joan took a similar approach, chiming in now and again and exchanging pleasantries with me.

I was exceedingly grateful that no one had pressured me to talk much. Only polite questions now and again. I guess it was a benefit that Declan hadn't been home in a while.

When dinner was done and dessert and coffee were served Joan said, "Now what are we going to do with Carman?"

Everyone groaned around the table.

"My wife fancies you're here to save us all from damnation," Brian Sr. said to me.

"You tell him, dear, tell him all of what's happened," Joan said to me.

Thank God for Declan. He spoke up and explained all that had occurred in the past few days and weeks leading up to here, ending with the strange feeling we had about the woods today.

"I told you, those woods there are as old as time itself. I'll bet you a faerie is what you saw. And a good thing too, they'll keep watch over you," Joan said.

Brian Sr. had a look like he'd rather his wife had lost her marbles than we were all telling the truth. The other kids seemed as if they were hanging onto every word Declan said. All were waiting for me to confirm the account Declan had just given.

"Yeah, I wish I could tell you it was all a lie but not a word he said isn't true," I said.

"I told you, Brian," Joan said. "Will you let her heal you now?"

"Heal him with what?" Rory chimed in.

"A ritual." Joan tilted her chin up at that.

"Where did you find this ritual?" Michael asked.

"Oh, for heaven's sake, it's only a healing ritual—some sage, say a few words, it's nothing. Pagan ritual. I think your father was cursed by that witch Carman,"

"Why though?" Siobhan said.

"The story goes to say that our wealth was cursed. Some woman your great-great-uncle had spited when he amassed his wealth took it personally that he didn't love her.

"She placed a curse on him and his kin that they were to be plagued by sickness all their days. Your uncle had a white witch reverse the curse and they rid the world of the woman.

"Only, a few weeks ago your father ran into a woman fetching his golf ball out of the woods. How odd he thought and so he told me that the young woman seemed to appear and disappear so quickly.

"Your father being a terrible golfer and an even worse cynic thought little of it, but I remembered the stories his mother used to tell. I did a little digging and found the name of the woman your uncle had defeated was Carman. And our lovely Bridget here is who will be defeating her."

Everyone looked dubiously at me.

"Bridget the smith will make a weapon of iron to defeat Carman, Bridget the healer will cure the sickness, and Bridget will protect us and be protected by the animals."

She said it all like a prophecy.

"When Declan called me about the dog following her all that time ago I thought instantly of Brigid. I told Declan to stick to her like glue, that she would need someone to help her.

"I wasn't sure that I was right at the time. And I had no idea your father would fall ill. But the same night that your father fell ill, that dog went to protect our Bridget here, and I knew I was right. Lucky me, the two of them enjoyed each other's company all this time," she said with a little twinkle in her eye.

"So, what do I do?" I said rather lamely as I blushed from the scrutiny of everyone.

Smiling broadly his mother reached across to pat my hand. "You'll know what to do, dear. But first, you'll help me with the tincture."

"I can do that," I said.

What the hell? At least her logic and the series of events coincided well enough to be plausible. Declan's family seemed to be thinking along the same lines I was. It was silent a few minutes before Joan spoke again.

"Well go on and finish your dessert everyone and then we'll get to work. I'll need the lot of you," she said.

Finishing dessert and carrying empty plates into the kitchen, Declan pulled me into the empty living room.

"Talk to me," he said.

"I think your family is lovely," I said.

"Thank you. Tell me what you're really thinking."

"By all accounts, Declan, your mother makes some sense. Damn it if I don't want her to make sense but she's explained the unexplainable. I have to humor the idea that she's right and go through with it."

"Good, I was hoping you would say that."

He kissed me entirely inappropriately for the venue and yet I knew I needed a kiss like that. There was a different type of feeling when you're the perpetual outsider, finally feeling like you belong somewhere. I was always odd, but they all were too, and we might be crazy but at least we were crazy together.

To my mortification, his mother peeked her head in as we were pulling apart. Hands still on my hips, Declan gave her a look.

"Well, you have time enough for that later. Let's get to work," she said.

"You heard her," Declan said, instructing me to follow her with a wave of his hand. He smacked my ass after his mother was out of the room and I cursed him silently. And then I took it back because curses were suddenly a lot more real than I thought.

In the kitchen, everyone was situated in different poses of disbelief and wonder. Siobhan was particularly intrigued, at the stove with her mother watching the happenings and holding the book the ritual was in.

"What do I do?" I said.

"Come stir the tincture, clockwise," Joan replied.

Taking my place at the stove I stirred it continuously as his mother added all types of different spices and ingredients. When she was finished adding ingredients she instructed me to read a few lines from the book.

Never having spoken or read Gaelic I could feel the blush reach my hairline as sweat broke out all over. I was not comfortable with talking in front of people at all, never mind in a foreign language.

Sure, I was a waitress, but you only ever talk to one table at a time and if it's a party, you usually don't address them at once.

Plus, you get used to it, it's always the same.

Tentatively saying the first few lines I found that I sounded convincing, at least to myself. Confidence coming from somewhere, Declan's hand on my shoulder reassured me more. Finishing the last my body was buzzing with electricity from the words and not Declan. I glanced up at him at the end.

He looked dumbfounded. Maybe amazed.

"Now what?" I said to Joan.

She was looking at me like the cat that got the cream.

"You *are* her," she whispered reverently.

Looking back at the rest of them, they all had the same look on their faces. I had only said a few words in Gaelic.

Glancing down in embarrassment I saw that the ingredients in the pot shimmered. Like a thousand fireflies were there and not spices. I chanced a glance at my hand. My skin looked similar to the tincture but much finer, a soft glow hovered over it.

"Now dear, let's bring this to Brian," Joan said.

Pouring the mixture into a mug, Joan instructed me through a series of other movements. All the while chanting the last line of the reading she told me to walk counterclockwise, point the cup in the direction of the setting sun, and other very ritualistic things. I and the mug glowed the whole time.

When all was said and done, Brian Sr. took a long drink of the mix and had a coughing fit as a result, making a face like I had given him poison instead of a healing draught.

"How do you feel, my love?" Joan said to Brian when he composed himself.

He stood up in answer to her question. Putting his hands out and spinning in a slow circle he stopped and stared at his wife. She had that look on her face again, this time infinitely smugger than the one she had given me.

"You old fool, doubting your wife," she said as she gave him a big kiss.

He had to bend over to reach her, making me think of the difference between Declan and me. Tears shone in both of their eyes as they pulled away. Joan turned a look of scorn on her family.

"You all will do well to listen to the ramblings of old women. Might learn a thing or two," she said.

Coming up to me, she took both of my hands in hers.

"Thank you dear for giving me my husband back. Don't you worry now, you did all well and good and when the time comes to face Carman you will again."

"Thank you," I said for lack of something better to say, glad at least she had confidence in me.

"Off with all of you now. It's time we're all off to bed," Joan said.

Pulling me into a big hug, she held on a few seconds and when she pulled back the tears were there again. I smiled back at her and grabbed her hand, a silent reassurance.

I can't imagine how she must have felt, not knowing whether she was crazy or not. Putting her faith in a woman she's never met halfway across the world.

I said as much to Declan when we were in the car.

"I agree. But she was right." He said the last with every bit of disbelief I felt.

"I suppose she was," I said quietly, looking at my hands.

I didn't have anything more to say after that and neither did Declan. Both lost in thought and more than a little tired we focused out the window on the dark countryside rolling by. The glow had faded after his dad drank the draught, but I kept glancing at my hands looking at them like they were alien.

Had my powers only turned on because a threat was now near, or had they always been capable? Trying to think of instances of healing in my past I came up blank. Maybe they needed the ritual to work?

So many questions with no answers popped up in my head. Tomorrow I would have to ask Joan more about what she knew.

Pulling into the courtyard of the house I was glad to see the house had lights on everywhere. Not wanting another run-in with Darkness, I was also glad to see Sid slink out from a corner near the carriage house that we'd left open for him.

All piling inside, Declan led the way to the living room. In the hearth, a fire already roared, and tea was set out for us. Helping me out of my coat, I asked Declan if I would ever see the elves he had running around doing these things for us.

"Tomorrow you will. Tommy and his wife Loretta live here and care for the property. They'll be making breakfast and the like. They're who run operations whether for an event like a wedding or as a bed-and-breakfast," he said.

"You don't have someone do that at home too do you?" I said as he hung up the coats and we each took a seat on the couch. Sid was laying by the fire.

"No, when it's just me I do things for myself. Of course, I could hire someone, and I do have a personal assistant, but she mostly sets appointments for me and things like that."

"She?" I said.

"Edna. Edna is in her fifties and very tech-savvy and she cleans the house whether I tell her to or not. She's who got your measurements for the clothes. You have no reason to be jealous, though I do like the look in your eyes right now."

"So are we going to talk about it?"

"Talk about what? That you glowed like a candle while thousands of tiny fireflies danced to the beat of your drum? That my mother's already married us in her head? Or that my father may have actually been healed?"

"Yes," was all I said.

"Well, what's there to say? I saw you speak Gaelic like it was your native tongue. I saw my father hale and hearty after being in a wheelchair. And watched my family fall in love with you too."

"I did speak it well, didn't I?"

"I'll tell you, Bridget, I had no confidence in your ability to speak Gaelic and at first you were rough but then you weren't."

"Something just took over once I got started."

"Magic, my love,"

"Magic," was all I said.

"Bridget, I spent a lifetime hearing my mom ramble on about

faeries and nymphs and all sorts of things that I said didn't exist. And then you come along and make me believe in things I never dreamed of before and I'm just as out of sorts as you."

"Well, I spent a lifetime thinking I was worthless and here I am doing magic." Stupid mouth, why did I say that?

"You were never worthless," he said softly.

Getting off the couch, Declan came over to kneel beside my seat, rendering him face to face with me. He put both giant hands on either side of my face.

"The people that made you feel that way did so because of their insecurities. You're one of the smartest, most talented, and kindest women I've had the pleasure to meet. Glowing like a glowworm notwithstanding."

"I thought that was my best feature."

"No, your best feature is your eyes."

He ran his hands down to my waist.

"And your ass," he added.

"Is that so?" I said.

"Yes," he said as he grabbed the hem of my dress and began to inch it up my legs.

* * *

The pretty undergarments didn't survive the night, but we did so I thought that was a good thing. I awoke without a stitch on, arms and legs tangled with Declan's in the master bedroom. The morning sun streamed in from everywhere it seemed, not having closed the curtains.

Declan didn't have a stitch on either and I thought that was also a good thing. Deciding to thank him for his kindness I woke him up.

Ambling down the stairs a while later, languid and sedated, the smell of coffee and bacon met us at the landing. I could get used to this. Grabbing Declan's hand I squeezed it to let him know I thought so. His returning smile was dazzling, all sleepy eyes and bedroom hair. He looked every bit the boy next door.

If the boy next door was a giant that is.

I sobered up when I remembered I would be meeting Tommy and Loretta this morning. Man, strangers before coffee, not my favorite.

We took our seats at the table. There were only two spots set. Coffee was already placed on the table, complete with fixings. Again, I thought I could get used to this.

Making our coffee, I took a few sips so that I could wake up some. The warmth spread through my veins as the caffeine went to work. It was delicious too, creamy and earthy without the bitterness cheap coffee can get.

We sat there in companionable silence, enjoying the coffee and the morning sunshine. I still couldn't get over the estate. It was so beautiful here. Declan was checking his phone.

When Loretta came in, I had enough coffee in my veins, and I was much more pleasant to be around. She came in holding two serving plates filled with food, one with muffins and pastries and the other with bacon and eggs.

"Good morning," she chirped, a bright smile on her aging face.

She was maybe in her fifties, graying hair pulled into a bun at the nape of her neck. Her face was kind, and she was tall and lean, looking like she spent her days doing labor. I could picture her in the gardens on the grounds pulling weeds with one of those hats on.

Declan said good morning and introduced us. They chatted a minute or two before she retreated to the kitchen with the promise to return to clean up.

"She seems lovely," I said.

"She is. You'll like her husband too. Especially after you're awake."

"Mmm." I grunted.

I had a theory that I was never fully awake but rather I sleep-walked through life fueled by caffeine. I started drinking coffee at only thirteen or so. The mornings getting ready at my mom's house were cold, and I wanted the coffee to warm me up while I did so.

Furthermore, working in a restaurant since age sixteen meant that I was more of a night owl. All of the action in restaurants happen late at night. And after hours. Which meant that school was way too early, and coffee was the only reason I survived.

Digging into the food I was surprised to find that I was starving. The two full plates that Loretta had brought in were nearly gone by the time we were through with them. There wasn't any time to talk for the pace I shoveled food into my mouth.

"Worked up an appetite?" Declan said with raised eyebrows.

"I guess. All that magic must have done it," I said giving him a lascivious look to hint at my double entendre.

"Ah yes, all the magic. I find I have a hearty appetite too this morning."

"Hmmm," I said. He had done some feats last night that would warrant an appetite.

"Well now that you've gotten mostly woken up, today I think we'll head back to my parents in the early afternoon and see what my mother has to say and then I'll take you out on the town."

"Sounds like a plan. Should we bring Sid?"

"We'll let him decide. Loretta and Tommy have no problem looking after him."

"Do they know what he is?" I whispered.

"Loretta seems dubious, but Tommy likes that he'll scare the rodents from digging up the garden and the landscaping."

"So she does garden. And how do you know?"

"I texted them about it before we came. I can tell by Loretta's mannerisms that she knows something is up. They've been with my family as long as I can remember. I used to play with their children when we would come here."

"Did they know your father had been sick?"

"Yes, though I don't know to what extent."

"Do they know about me?"

"No, I don't think so. But they've never met a girlfriend of mine, so they are very curious I'm sure. Outside of their daughter," he added the last a little more rushed.

"You dated their daughter?"

"In high school. It was ages ago, and it wasn't a serious relationship. It was right around when my father went off the rocker. But I'm with you now and don't forget it."

He knew me too well. Tamping down my insecurities I said, "Yes, you are. And I have little intention of letting you go."

There, that was smooth! And not at all an inappropriate response to something silly like a high school girlfriend. I only hoped we didn't run into her.

"You don't fool me for a second, you know. Even though you have nothing to worry about anyway."

Damn.

"It was a good attempt though. Next time don't look like you might kill me."

"I might though."

"I know. That's why you have nothing to worry about."

"Because you're afraid of me?"

"No lass, because nothing gets my heart rate up more than when you look fierce as you do right now."

"Oh?" I said, my heart rate picking up at that.

"And nothing melts my heart like when you look all vulnerable underneath all of that bravado."

"Oh." I was a little dejected at that. I preferred fierce to vulnerable.

"Like right now when you're worrying your bottom lip over being vulnerable," he said, reaching a hand out to cup my jaw.

"I don't do vulnerable."

"You do with me."

"Not willingly."

"Not all the time but sometimes."

I didn't have anything to say about that. It seems I did do vulnerable with him. That's why I got so defensive about silly things. I was in too deep, and I couldn't bear the idea he might change his mind about me.

The moment was over when Loretta came back in with Tommy to get the empty dishes, bringing orange juice with them. Could they be any more perfect? Quenching my thirst, Declan introduced me to Tommy, and we all chatted for a bit, complimenting them on everything and thanking them numerous times.

Whether it is someone's job or not, thanks are always appreciated. It was evident that the pair took their jobs seriously and felt lucky to have jobs that allowed them so much freedom. I could understand why, never liking authority myself. I preferred bosses that allowed me liberties and found I worked better that way.

Tommy and Loretta took pride in what they did, so the thanks were sincerely appreciated. I'm certain they were compensated handsomely for their services as well. And their warmth told of a lifetime of love, toward Declan and each other.

Tommy seemed the talker of the two, though he was behind the scenes, cooking, and other things. Loretta was talkative enough but observant, good front-of-house qualities. It's one thing to do as a boss says and another to anticipate their needs. Loretta was proving to be the latter.

I understood what Declan meant now too. Loretta's keen intuition had her radar up, and she was trying to put the puzzle together. Though pleasant, the wheels were turning in her head.

Thankfully, she seemed to acknowledge that I was not a threat as she warmly hugged me as well as Declan goodbye for the day after Declan said we would not return until late and therefore they could have the day to themselves.

"Loretta would probably have been thrilled if you married her daughter," I said when we were upstairs.

"They both would have. As would my parents have been and probably so would Lynn, their daughter," he said.

"So why not?"

"Lynn is sweet as honey like her mother. Beautiful too, smart, really a lovely girl and a great match."

"Yea she sounds peachy," I said, scorn evident.

"Shame, I like my women with a little spice," he said as he wrapped my legs around him and laid me on the bed.

Laying his big body on top of me, my legs wrapped around his waist, his face inches from mine.

"She's not you," he said, and he kissed me thoroughly.

❋ ❋ ❋

"I won't be able to walk if we keep up this pace," I said when we were in the car.

"Good, then I can have you all to myself," he said.

He already did whether he knew it or not.

Sitting back in the seat I watched the world go by as he drove. I was probably the happiest I had ever been in my life, and yet a death threat loomed over my head. All that lovemaking left me in a haze of contentment, not even imminent death could penetrate. At least I would die sated and with a smile on my face.

Sid stayed behind. After session number whatever we had showered and dressed. Sid was outside when we got in the car and Declan held the door open for him a while until Sid trotted away to do whatever it was he did.

I was in too deep and for once I think I liked it. I genuinely hadn't wanted to date Declan before. Our friendship was perfect why mess with it? But now I know the real reason was fear. I was afraid of the implications. I think I knew once we got started there was no stopping this. Good thing too because I didn't want to stop.

Staring out the window I thought of everything that had led me to here. Everything I thought would break me that didn't. All the heartbreak and the confusion. It all made sense when you got there, even if it never did while you were going through it. Even if here wasn't a final destination it was a good pit stop at least.

Declan and I wouldn't have been friends first for so long

before getting together if it wasn't for all the heartbreak. We wouldn't have fought for each other if we didn't think the other was worth it.

And we wouldn't be able to laugh at things many relationships are broken over like jealousy. For better or worse I trusted Declan on a level I hadn't ever trusted another human being and I was certain he wouldn't abuse that trust. It's pretty cool when you think of it that way.

"I am your girlfriend, right?" I blurted out, realizing we had never actually said it.

"No, I have no time for a girlfriend."

"That's not exactly the answer I anticipated."

"I have no time for a girlfriend; I intend for you to be my wife."

"I also was not prepared for that answer."

He laughed out loud at that one.

"Yes, you're my girlfriend for now. I only hope you know it's a title I don't intend to keep for you for long."

"I think I could be down with that."

"You think?"

"Well if you're so rich it better be a big ring is all I'm saying."

"Oh, don't worry about that. Everything is big with me," he said with a wink.

"Don't I know it," I said, raising my eyebrows.

He laughed again, and I thought I might like to hear that sound for a lifetime.

# CHAPTER 9

We were the only ones with his parents today. Everyone else was back to their lives, crisis having been averted, for now. Receiving warm hugs from them both, I started to feel hope that things would be alright. The fact that Sid felt it was alright to leave me be for now was a good sign too.

That hope only made me more nervous though and there were fewer people between me and his parents to act as buffers. I started getting way too in my head looking at his parents as my future in-laws.

Declan noticed and grabbed my hand and I remembered why I was thinking of accepting them as my future in-laws. It's always a package deal, isn't it?

Joan had tea and lunch waiting for us on the table since it was early afternoon. Ushering us over she took a seat next to me and patted my hand.

"So good to see you again, dear. Last night was a lot of excitement. I'm looking forward to getting to know you better. I can't thank you enough for your helping us," she said.

"It was no problem, really," I said.

It wasn't since I didn't know what I did exactly.

"Oh no problem for you, of course!"

"I guess not," I said dubiously.

"Right, Declan said you don't really know why you have these powers. Well, I can't say for sure but the reason we name anyone after saints and the like is that you want your babe to take on the qualities of that saint. You must have magic in your blood is all. And you have to be open to it too."

"Open to it how?"

"Faith in something more ought to do it. Like myself, I always teased the kids about faeries, to be sure, but a small part of me believed they were real. It's quite like believing in God. You can't see Him, but you believe He is real. Miracles happen that way."

The logic was there.

"Eat dear," she said as she continued. "I know Declan's told me of your intelligence and your insight. If you ask me I think you never quite fit in because you don't. Like an eagle among turkeys, you were meant to fly while everyone else can't. Quite like my Declan if you ask me."

She said the last more conspiratorially. The men had been in conversation with each other and paid us no mind. I think Joan wanted it that way.

"So what do I do?" I said.

"Nothing dear. You can study and prepare yourself, but your true calling will find you when the time comes,"

"Are you sure? It feels like I should be going to school or something,"

"No, but what are we ever sure about? I'm as sure as I am about anything else, and I like to think my intuition has done me well."

"I can agree with that," I said, having been a part of her intuition myself.

"He won't hurt you, by the way, dear. He's never looked at anyone the way he looks at you," she said softly.

I didn't know what to say to that, so I looked at Declan.

"I know," I said after a beat.

"Promise me the same."

"Promise," I said, reaching out to touch her arm.

I did promise. I had no intentions of hurting Declan. Only, I knew from experience that even with the best of intentions people still got hurt. But Joan knew that.

Joan was incredibly disarming. She had a knack for getting right to the heart of things. I didn't want to, but I felt like I could tell her anything and she would never judge me.

"Now when we're done here, I have a few things for you before you go," she said.

Agreeing, we finished our lunch and chatted about how I liked the house we were staying at and other things. She answered most of my questions.

Like how I had magic in my blood and so did her family. Of course, there was no way to really know, but she gave me examples like how my gut instinct was usually right and how I knew things I shouldn't sometimes.

Elaborating on a few of the faerie types she mentioned that I should practice listening to that voice. That most of the faeries I would encounter near the old house would be there to help me and I should try to listen. But Carman and her three sons would have a hard time near the house because it had a lot of the old magic in the woods and lake.

Leaving the men after we finished eating, she led me to the kitchen where she had left the items she wanted to give me. On the counter were three green mesh bags and what looked like a necklace.

Grabbing the necklace first, she clasped it around my neck. It was a sturdy silver chain with a Celtic knot as the pendant on it

"For protection," she said.

Grabbing one mesh bag she said, "This one is filled with herbs. It has sage for cleansing, dill for protection, and oregano for good luck. Keep it in your coat pocket,"

Placing that one in my hand she grabbed another. "This one has thyme. It'll help you talk to the faeries and the other realm for help if you need it. I would keep this one on you at all times."

Taking a bracelet with different colored stones as charms out of the last one she told me about them one at a time. "Aquamarine, it's supposed to be a calming stone. Said to protect sailors from drowning, release attachments and heal emotional issues. It'll grant you favor with good spirits who will help you. Sharpen your intuitions.

"Emerald for guidance, heliodor for magic and manifestation, serpentine for the luck of the Irish. It'll bring you abundance. That last one will help you get control of your spirituality too. Quartz for healing. Healers need healing too. And finally, peridot will clear negativity and cleanse your mind, body, and spirit."

Handing me that bag she looked at me seriously.

"Keep that one on you at all times. During the full moon leave it on the nightstand by the bed, preferably in the full moonlight. It will enhance the powers. I've also instructed Loretta to place rue, mugwort, and yarrow at the doors to ward off witches and evil spirits. She put salt on the windowsills too. Evil can't cross lines of salt so here." She grabbed a saltshaker from a cabinet and handed it to me. "Keep that in your coat too."

"Thank you, I appreciate your thoughtfulness," I said.

"That shaker ought to be enough for one small circle for Declan and you but here." She grabbed a large container of salt used to refill shakers. "Keep that one handy too. Of course, there's one at the house so keep that one in the car and I'll ask Loretta to put salt in the bedroom."

"We can pick up salt when we leave, no need to take yours," I said handing hers back.

"Nonsense! I'm not curing anything at the moment. I do not need all that salt," she said with a wink telling me she was teasing.

"I can't thank you enough. I appreciate your worrying about me, truly. Is there some way I could repay you?" I said.

I was bad at accepting help or allowing people to be nice to me. Usually, people were only nice because they wanted something. Joan didn't strike me that way and I never knew how to handle it.

And if she told Loretta all of this before this morning it would explain why Loretta was suspicious. Probably thought I was a witch, and I had made the whole family do my bidding. Placing salt in the bedroom, my goodness.

"You already have, dear. You gave me my husband and my son back. I've never seen Declan happier, truth be told, and I have you to thank for that," she said, tears shining in her eyes.

"My Declan," she continued. "Never did know what to do with

that one. So serious, so difficult, so *smart*. Not that the rest of us aren't. But my Declan always wanted *more.*

"Suppose he gets it from me, but he always wanted more than anyone could give him. I may have met only a girlfriend or two, though I know there were more. But he was always so aloof. Lost in the businesses he was building, attached to the computer. I think he just liked the company. He was awful lonely. Especially after my Siobhan joined us.

"You changed all of that. The minute he laid eyes on you he called me up telling me all about you. He started calling me daily to talk about you. 'No, Mom, we're just friends,' he would say. Both lying to yourselves you were. I know the dog had something to do with it at first but to tell you the truth he forgot about that once he got to know you. He tried to remember it was about the dog but most days he only wanted to tell me stories about you.

"Now, I don't say this to embarrass either of you. I only say it as an old woman who's seen a lot more than the two of you. You both have something special, something very few people ever find but everyone looks for. Appreciate it, and each other. This life is too short, don't let silly things get in the way," she said, letting out a deep sigh when she was done.

"Did you two never have much of a relationship?"

"There's that insight. Yes, dear, of all my babies Declan gave me the hardest time. Ever since you, he's talked to me more than I think he spoke to me in the thirty years I raised him.

"I know he had the toughest time when Brian had his troubles, and I blame myself for that. Love our Siobhan we do, but she was late to the party. I sometimes wish I could have had her ten years earlier, but I suppose God has a plan after all. Even if you don't always get to know it when you think you need to."

"No, I don't suppose you do. Guess that takes half the fun out of it if you knew what was in store."

"Isn't that the truth? Well, enough ramblings for you today. Just know you've made quite an impact on our little family, and I am forever grateful to you for that."

"I should be the one thanking you. I think it's Declan and you that saved me," I said softly.

"You two saved each other," she said matter-of-factly, successfully winning the argument.

Squeezing my hand she carried the salt back to the table where the men were, handing it to Declan with instructions to keep it in the car. He gave both of us a look and she explained its uses.

"Bridget is fully stocked now. Last thing I'll give her is a book where most of the incantations can be found but I left that in the hall, so we'll grab that on your way out. Here Declan, this is for you." She reached into her pocket and pulled out a necklace similar to mine but more masculine.

Clasping it around his neck she kissed him on the cheek when she was done.

"Protection for you too," she said smiling at him.

"And where's yours?" Declan asked her.

She revealed a bracelet with the pendant, instructing Brian to do the same.

"I've gotten us all one so the evil spirits and such have a harder time next time," she said.

He smiled at that and stood, kissing her on the cheek as he did so.

"Good. Lunch was wonderful Mom, thank you," he said, his deep voice warm with emotion.

"Always my pleasure, dear. Now go show your lady a fun time. I'm determined she enjoy herself some now that she is better protected," she said, ushering us to the front door.

Brian shook Declan's hand and deciding it wasn't enough he wrapped his son in a bear hug. Turning his attention to me, he did the same, whispering a fervent, "thank you," as he did so. Men can always say a lot more in fewer words than women, I mused.

Joan gave us goodbyes next, with warm hugs and kisses on the cheeks. She squeezed my hand one last time as she did so and shooed us out the door, book in Declan's hands. As Irish goodbyes went that was fairly quick. My family said goodbye for a minimum of a half-hour every time.

"What's on the agenda?" I said when we were in the car.

"It's a surprise. You could tell me why my mom was so teary though."

"She loves you."

"It's more than that."

"Isn't it always? Let's just say I guess I made you soft."

"Ha, you? Maybe in comparison."

"To who?!"

"Yourself! Woman, you're daft if you think you're all sentimental and mushy."

"I am sometimes," I said feeling a little mushy now.

"You're made of steel and it's just how I like you. Lesser women crumble under the pressures you brush off. Walking through fire like you were water. Quite admirable in fact."

"Hmm. I like it when you say it that way."

"Besides a woman couldn't be with a man like me if she wasn't of sound mind and body."

"Oh, yeah, you're a real tough guy."

"See what I mean? You never noticed how people cowed when I walked in the door. Not my girl, you stared me down. Just saw me for me. Watch today, watch people stare at me like an ogre."

"People do not stare at you like an ogre. And I have noticed you have a presence when you walk in the room."

"When? At the pet store when I told you my net worth? Sweetheart, I saw the change in your face, and you know what I saw? Wonder, maybe a little hero worship..." He gave me a wink there. "But no fear."

"Why would I fear you?"

"Exactly, why would *you*? My love, like it or not, you've the countenance of a regular ice queen. If I didn't know you better I'd be terrified of you."

"You would not. No one scares you."

"You do lass. Just not in the way you mean it," he said softly. "I only hope I never piss you off enough for you to write me off. I have a feeling it would be my death sentence,"

"You couldn't do anything bad enough to deserve it, Declan," I said grabbing his hand. "You're too soft."

That got a bark of laughter out of him as I had intended it to.

"Aye, for you maybe I am," he said as he threaded his fingers through mine.

He thinks I'm tough, huh? I suppose I was in a way, but I rarely thought of myself that way. Maybe it's just that I knew how much anxiety I felt all the time. You can't be tough and anxious. Funny how people view you differently than you see yourself.

"What did she give you? Besides the necklace," he asked after a moment.

"Yes, necklace, bracelet of crystals, a bag of herbs, a bag of thyme, and a saltshaker."

"A saltshaker?"

"For a circle of salt, you know, keep the evil spirits out?"

"You do know?"

"I mean, yeah, I've always loved all the supernatural things, so I wasn't surprised at your mom's reasoning and what she picked."

He just glanced at me.

"Well, there's this show I always loved, called *Supernatural* actually, and a lot of the show was done according to the true legends it depicted. I know because I fact-checked them because I'm a nerd. And so that, combined with my general nerdiness, I guess I already have a working knowledge of these kinds of things."

"I suppose I shouldn't be surprised. A woman I can debate philosophy with would have an open enough mind to accept crystals as having supernatural capabilities," he said.

"They do as long as you believe. Whether it's the crystal itself or the placebo effect is somewhat irrelevant."

We'd once had an intense debate surrounding existentialism. If nothing matters are there ever lines that get crossed? When does it matter?

Of course, things mattered, but we both agreed only you assigned meaning to things. There were few inherently meaningful things. And whether you were headed toward a destination or not, you'd never know so you had to cherry-pick as you went along, making the next best move like chess.

Pulling off the main road and into a drive I saw a castle up ahead and my heart leaped.

"A castle! Declan is that where we're going? Please tell me that's where we're going?"

"Yes, of course it's where we're going. I could hardly bring you to Ireland and not to a castle."

Jumping up in my seat I kissed him on the cheek as I continued to thank him. It was a lifelong dream of mine to see a castle in Ireland. I couldn't wait to touch everything I was allowed to and imagine the many lives the castle walls held.

"You're more excited to see a castle than when I told you I loved you, told you I was filthy rich, or when I bought you fancy clothes," he said.

"Well, you'll be telling me you love me for a long time to come, clothes never did much for me, and I would love you if you were dirt poor. It won't be every day I get to see a castle though." I meant every word.

"You aren't wrong," he said, holding my hand a little tighter.

Continuing up the windy drive to the castle at a slow pace I was bouncing out of my seat. It was true, I liked money and the fancy things it allowed you to have but I liked it more for the experiences.

This was one experience, in particular, I was grateful for. But if we were dirt poor and I couldn't do this, I would be fine. Declan is worth more than a castle.

This was definitely the most romantic and sweetest thing anyone had ever done for me though. So when he parked I let him know how much I appreciated it and him.

Kissing him all over his face and hugging him until he pushed me away I thought I had accurately expressed my appreciation, for now. The rest would have to wait as it wasn't publicly appropriate.

"What's the name?" I asked as we made our way to the keep.

"Castlekirk, it's an O'Connor castle," he said.

"You're kidding!"

"I'm not, this is a genuine castle of the O'Connor clan."

"Can you trace your lineage to here?"

"Yes, we can. It trails off right around the cursed uncle though. That's why we think maybe he made good with the clan here. Possibly having a different surname or just becoming important within the clan."

"I'm jealous. I can only date back to right before my great grandparents emigrated to the United States."

"We can do that another time if you like. Or I can have someone trace it for you."

"I might like to have a hand in it. At least be able to see certain documents. Like someone's birth certificate that I know the parents would have touched."

"I agree."

Walking up to the castle I was itching to get inside. Imagining the lives of people hundreds of years ago fascinated me beyond measure. There was just something so simple and yet so complicated about those times. Everything could kill you and everything took an immense amount of labor and time to produce.

And yet they did it. They fetched water and boiled it, and felled trees and chopped wood for the fire. But then that was it; there wasn't much time for other stuff. It was work and church.

Maybe I just mourned the simplicity. The world today is so fast. There's a different appreciation for life when everything you get is hard to come by. I liked the not dying at thirty part, though.

Trying to picture the lives that had passed through I was imagining Declan's uncle. A love affair gone wrong or simply unrequited love? I wondered if this was where it had all transpired.

Thinking of Declan in a kilt made me laugh a little. Declan caught my laughter and gave me a look.

"You in a kilt," I said.

"I have one if you'd like to see me in it." He winked, and I thought it wouldn't be so bad after all.

Then again I couldn't imagine him looking bad in anything. His square jaw, broad shoulders, and those green eyes you could drown in. His reddish hair was tousled today, windswept out in the open of the courtyard. Thinking of him in a kilt with nothing underneath was something I would be alright with.

"Can we do that later?" I asked.

His answering laughter was wonderful.

"I think we can lass," he said as he patted my butt.

This was too much fun. Life with Declan could be alright.

*　*　*

Finishing the tour I felt grateful. Just in awe of the human condition. All the love and laughter that must have passed through these walls. And the hardship. It really put things in perspective like nothing else I had seen yet.

Maybe only the Metropolitan Museum of Art in New York City could compare. Seeing the ancient Egyptian relics and the Mesopotamian exhibits did trump these castles but only in age not in grandeur. Only because they were in a glass case where I was in the castle.

The castle was a total immersion into the daily lives of the inhabitants. It made me wish I could live like they did if only for a little while.

I held Declan's hand the whole time, an anomaly for me. I'm affectionate but holding hands always felt obnoxious. How did people do it comfortably? But comfortable or not I couldn't thank Declan enough and holding his hand was my way of showing appreciation for him.

Walking toward the car in a content silence I was absorbing the last few minutes I would have at the castle. Picturing men, women, and children out here in period clothing doing their chores.

Maybe the kids were playing, and dogs were roaming around. It looked picturesque in my head, though I knew it wasn't as clean as I was imagining it.

Something skittered past in my peripheral vision. Only kind of seeing a shape I turned my head, but I didn't see anything. My adrenaline had spiked though, and I was rooted to the ground scanning the grounds for something, only I didn't know what.

"What is it, Bridget?" Declan said, noticing I had frozen.

"I'm not sure, I thought I saw something."

Something warm met my hand, and I shrieked. Looking down I saw Sid. He had slunk right alongside me, tail tucked and bristling. I guess I was more spooked than I thought.

Wait, we hadn't brought Sid.

Looking at Declan with alarm I noticed he realized it too. This means Sid didn't think things were entirely cool over here. The question was, was it Sid I saw or something else?

"What do we do?" I asked.

"I'm not completely sure," Declan answered.

Glancing around at the other people in the courtyard, no one seemed the least bit concerned about us or anything else for that matter. They were looking at Declan like he was an ogre, and some were looking at Sid.

But mostly on their faces was curiosity and a bit of intimidation at both of their sizes. Some people ogled at my smallness to their largeness but mostly I was ignored.

One face stood out of the crowd, one man staring at me with glittering dark eyes. He was handsome in a movie star kind of way. If the movie star was also in and out of rehab.

His lazy smile beckoned me to him, leaning back against a stone wall, arms crossed in nonchalance. When he caught my eye, he got up and started toward me.

"Who's that?" Declan asked following my line of sight.

"My ex," I said dumbly.

Declan bristled immediately. He'd caught the tail end of that relationship at the beginning of our friendship and to say that I was a wreck would be an understatement. Nick was a liar, a cheat, and all-around abusive.

But he was good at it. Very good at it.

He rarely left marks and if he did, they were in places easily hidden. And in the morning he was so apologetic I almost believed him.

For lack of brain cells, when Nick approached me and hugged me, I hugged him back. It was a part of his charm; he could be so disarming.

"Bridget, it's good to see you. What are you doing here?" Nick said.

"Uh," I said, completely flabbergasted.

"She's with me," Declan chimed in, all masculine energy permeating my stupidity. His face was etched in stone, but I saw through to how angry he really was. Damn it, why was I rooted to the ground?

"Yes! Nick this is Declan, my boyfriend," I said finally, stumbling only a little on the last word.

Stupid, Bridget! Get it together!

"Nice to meet you," Nick said, dismissing Declan altogether.

He always thought he was better than everyone. And not in the pissing contest way—he genuinely didn't think there *was* any competition.

"Why are you here?" I said after a second.

"Just visiting," Nick said, vague, avoiding the real question.

Why are you anywhere near *me*?

"Well, it was nice to see you, Bridget. You look lovely as ever," Nick said, kissing me on the cheek as he sauntered away.

Blinking after a second or two of staring at his back, I looked up to see a very irritated Declan. Shit.

"I'm sorry, I don't know what just happened," I said to him.

"You just drooled all over your piece-of-shit ex is what you did," Declan spat.

"No! I didn't! I just was shocked to see him."

"You didn't seem too upset to see him."

"I mean, I didn't feel anything but shock. What are the odds of seeing someone from your past halfway around the world?"

Declan just shook his head and stormed off toward the car.

"Declan!" I shouted after him, jogging to catch up.

Getting in the car, he slammed the door behind him and started it, white knuckles at ten and two. I let Sid in the back seat before quietly taking my own seat on the passenger side.

"Declan, I don't..." I started before he cut me off.

"You don't what, Bridget? Mean anything you say?" he spat.

"What the fuck are you talking about?" I said, temper flaring.

"You know what I'm talking about," he said as he was backing the car out of the spot.

"No! I don't! Explain it to me!" I was shouting now, never a good sign. Temper in the red now.

"Giving him a hug like your long-lost pal. D'ya forget what he treated you like?" His accent got thicker when he was mad.

"No! I just don't know. My brain shorted out! I just went temporarily stupid,"

"Stupid is right," he spat.

"Declan. Be reasonable. There's no reason we can't still enjoy our day out. Please just let it go, it didn't mean anything."

"Didn't mean anything? Why don't you just go give Nick another hug?"

"What!? No! What is wrong with you!?"

"You! Lousy girlfriend, you are, you know that?"

That one stung a bit and tears sprung in my eyes. *Well, that lasted long* I thought bitterly. *Already managed to screw this up, new record for me.*

Refusing to let him see I stared out the window as they silently streamed down my face. Fucking asshole.

Silently fuming the rest of the way home, I thought of everything that had transpired with Nick. When I met him he did a lot of romantic things like Declan.

We met in college. He was in one of my classes and immediately we clicked. After getting my number he would message me first thing every morning and the last thing every night no matter what.

Every day we had classes on the same day he would wait for

me in between classes to walk me to my next class or my car. He would come to the college to have lunch with me on his days off. There were surprise flowers and jewelry, holding doors open for me, carrying my books, pulling out all the stops.

Little did I know he was also seeing his ex when he would drop me off at class. Just friends my ass. He would leave me at my class to go walk her to hers.

My family never liked him, and I couldn't see it until little inconsistencies started popping up. Like my girlfriends showing me pictures of him partying on Facebook, pictures he had blocked me from being able to see.

Saying he was working late but his car was at home. Because obviously my best friend would encourage me to drive by to see for myself.

And still, I kept going back. It was hard to join the malicious bastard he was with the sweet gentleman he had displayed in the beginning.

Narcissism at its finest.

All of that wasn't even the half of it. It was the millions of ways he cut me down every chance he could. The verbal abuse eventually escalated to physical abuse when he was drunk and in the mood for a fight.

Too bad I was always ready for a fight.

But people accept the love they think they deserve. Nick wasn't the worst narcissist I had known.

The best ones hide in plain sight.

Hence why it was the type of relationship I was used to having. I continued to attract people like Nick because the worst narcissist of them all shared a roof with me my entire life. And still no one believed me about them.

By the bitter end with Nick, I felt used, stupid, and worthless. It was after months of misery I sobered up, had enough wallowing in self-pity, and in came Declan.

He started working with me right around the end of that whole shit show and we had chatted about it a bit. In reality, I understood Declan hating Nick, but I still didn't deserve to be treated like that, never again.

I still had one jealous person I couldn't appease. I wasn't about to add to the list. At least I had some distance from my family since I had moved out.

Distance didn't keep them from talking about me, spreading their lies as far and wide as they could. But the distance at least helped me stay out from the bottom of the bottle. And out of strangers' beds.

I had started spending all of my spare time with Declan. Now what would I do?

When we pulled up to the house, he stormed in, and I let him. Fuck him. It wasn't my fault.

Maybe I was better off. He probably would've cut and run once we started digging into my past anyway. Declan could do better than me. I was damaged goods.

Standing outside letting Sid do what Sid does, I stared over the loch to the dark woods beyond. Remembering my trinkets from this morning at his parents' house I took the thyme out and asked for the faeries to help me. This morning felt a world away.

Declan came back outside with a suitcase.

"The place is yours," he said and drove off.

Too stubborn to be berated for something so juvenile, I let him. Whatever man, if this is the beginning of the end it was fun while it lasted.

See? I knew we shouldn't have gotten involved. These things always went this way.

Deciding a walk would be lovely I set my sights on the woods beyond the lake. It was a ways away but doable if I hugged the shore. If any faeries were going to answer my call I imagined they were there.

❃ ❃ ❃

I arrived at my parents still seeing red. For lack of somewhere better to go, I landed here, a little confused at the last hour or so.

My mother met me at the front door, having heard the car door slam most likely.

"Declan?" she said, confusion evident.

I pushed past her into the house, heading straight for a glass of water in the kitchen. Not knowing what to do I thought that was a good enough place to start. Already with glass in hand, my mother came rushing into the kitchen with my dad, both being disturbed by my abrupt presence.

"Declan, where's Bridget?" my mum asked.

"At the house,"

"Ok. Why? Weren't you going to the castle?"

"We did."

"So weren't you going to take her to dinner after?"

"I was, but that was before she was all over her ex who conveniently showed up there."

"What?"

"Her ex who was miraculously there at the castle? Yeah, before that asshole."

"Well I don't know, Declan, but I can hardly believe Bridget planned something like that. After all, I'm the one who called you to come here last second. And why would she do that anyway?"

"I guess she's still hung up on him. I don't know, ma. Quit bugging me. I just want to be left alone."

"You come in my house tearing through like a bull in a china shop and you want me to leave you alone? I won't do it Declan. This doesn't make sense. She's mad about you and you her. Just this morning you were ready to marry the girl and now you're done with her?"

Some fog started to clear when she said that. I was ready to marry her this morning. What did happen?

"Declan?" my mom prompted.

"I told you. Her ex..."

"Well, what about him? That he was there? If that's all you've got on the girl you have a lot of apologizing to do if you ask me."

"She hugged him..."

"And?"

And...what? Was that all that I had against her? Some more fog cleared away.

"And I got really mad." I said.

"So you got mad because she hugged someone she used to date?" my mom said, smacking my bicep for being a fool.

"Declan, where'd your necklace go?" she said.

Touching my neck I couldn't find it. I shook my shirt out, checked my pants, the floor, my shoes, no necklace. I'd remember if I took it off...

"I don't know," I said, realization dawning on me.

The same conclusion shone in my mother's eyes.

"He took it. Evil if you ask me," she said. "You have to go get Bridget. He's certain to have taken hers too."

Giving my mom a kiss I hurried to the door. What an ass I'd made of myself. What an ass I had been to Bridget. God my poor Bridget didn't need any more heartache. She'd had more than enough and here I went proving all of her fears right. Damn it.

"Wait!" my mom called after me.

Rushing up to me, she pulled my sleeve up, sharpie marker in hand.

"What are you doing?" I asked.

"Protecting you," she said as she began drawing the Celtic knot that had been on the necklace. Taking her bracelet she formed a perfect, albeit sloppy, rendering of the knot on my forearm. Placing the marker in my hand she kissed me on my cheek.

"Do the same to Bridget once you get to her," she said as I ran out the door.

* * *

Walking along the water's edge I wished I could jump in. I had a love for swimming, but the air and water were far too cold for that.

As it was, I had made my way around the water's edge and

was nearly to the woods by now, the crisp air a balm for my emotions that were still quietly rioting inside.

I had grown up going to a lake where my stepmother's family owned property at for generations. Going there was like nothing else. It was the ultimate peace and relaxation. Except for the company I guess but you couldn't have it all could you?

Shrugging off more old wounds, I focused on the open one that was currently bleeding. Why did Declan have to be an ass too? Looking toward the woods ahead I saw something shimmer in the water in my peripheral vision.

A second later something grabbed hold of my foot, and before I could react cold water engulfed me.

With lightning speed, I was dragged underwater. Holding my breath to keep from inhaling the freezing water I opened my eyes to see green murkiness everywhere. Growing up swimming in a lake gave me an advantage I thought, to be able to orient myself a little.

Seaweed streamed past underneath me, and above the sunlight weakly penetrated in green ribbons slicing through the water. This meant I was further down than I would like to be.

Whatever had my ankle was colder than the water. I twisted enough to see a shimmering tail near my abdomen, vigorously moving, propelling us deeper.

My lungs were protesting but so far I was still lucid. Thinking as quickly as I could I reached out and grabbed stalks of seaweed as it flew by. Most were merely ripped out of the lake floor but every so often I would get a stronger one that would slow us down.

"Quit that," the creature said, whipping around to face me.

I think it was the mermaid thing, half-man, half-fish. It was ugly, with green skin and hair, fish eyes, and gills. It reminded me of the selkie from the lake at Declan's house.

It had worked though. I quit thrashing, but so did the thing.

Staring at me like I was the weird one it said, "How are you doing this?"

"What?" I said, equally flabbergasted.

As soon as I did, something quick came flying through the water and crashed into the creature, effectively breaking the grasp it had on me. I didn't waste any time getting away, swimming upwards as quickly as I could. After a second or two though, whatever had attacked the selkie was underneath me. Only this time it was carrying me to the surface.

※ ※ ※

Arriving back at the house much quicker than I ever thought possible, I couldn't see Bridget anywhere. Throwing the car in park I ran for the front door when I heard barking coming from the lake.

Turning around I saw Sid pacing back and forth at a spot a ways away on the shoreline. He was near the woods on the opposite side, barking like a madman. Deciding it would take far too long to get there on foot I jumped back into the car and tore across the grass, grateful for my SUV.

As I neared the spot where Sid was furiously pacing something came out of the water.

Was that a fucking horse?

※ ※ ※

As I broke the water's surface, I grabbed a firm hold on the mane that was beneath me.

Was this a fucking horse?

It was a damn horse. I mean I knew they could tread water, but I was fairly certain they couldn't dive like this one had just done.

Sid was at the water's edge losing his shit, stopping abruptly when he saw me and turned to his left. Following his line of sight I saw Declan tearing up the lawn on his way to me.

Coming to a stop near us he threw the door open and sprinted over to me as the horse finally trotted his way onto land. The horse continued on though, with Declan and Sid trailing after us before stopping at the tree line, further away from the water's edge.

When the horse came to a full stop I dismounted, patting his neck, and giving him a hug for saving me. He responded by nuzzling me before eating grass at a patch near us.

Before we could compare notes a shrill scream came from near the lake. Standing there in obvious agitation was a tall woman, her thin figure clad in black, with straight black hair nearly down to her hips. Her pale skin was flushed red with anger as she screamed again, advancing toward us.

Pulling a small bag out of her pocket she held it to her lips and started speaking in what I could only assume was ancient Gaelic. As she did so, the man Declan had called Darkness came sauntering out from the shadows of the trees nearer the lake. If he was there the whole time I had never seen him.

He was joined after a beat by two other men who I had not seen before but could assume were Evil and Violence, making the woman Carman. Neurons started firing in my brain. This recent episode must have been Violence's attempt at my life, but I survived.

Remembering the stones, Joan had said aquamarine was said to protect sailors from drowning. And the thyme. I had whispered to the thyme before I went on my walk, asking the faeries for help. It must have done something.

Reaching for my necklace I was going to ask it for protection, only it wasn't there. Looking at Declan I was about to tell him so when he pulled a sharpie marker out of his pocket and started drawing on my wrist. He was holding his forearm next to mine and was copying the Celtic knot he had drawn there.

"Gone. My mom thinks it was Evil that took them off us. Known as Nick."

"Nick?" I said, almost laughing.

"Comical isn't it? I think you were still somewhat protected by the stones but once I lost the necklace Evil was able to drive the wedge right between us."

"Separate us and go after me first."

"Except we were one step ahead," he said, kissing my palm as he finished his crude drawing on my wrist.

Both of us turning to face the four of them again, they had stopped their advance. As Carman stopped speaking to whatever was in her hand, a strange sensation went through me. Like thousands of needles were pricking me, except it was a dull sensation. Almost like they couldn't get past my clothing.

"Do you feel that?" I asked Declan.

"Like needles?"

"Yeah, that." I was thoroughly confused, but I didn't know what to do.

Looking around me for a weapon of some sort, I noticed Sid and the horse stood stock-still behind us, facing our foes but fairly relaxed. Even more confused I started to wonder why they were so nonplussed.

We were in the woods. The horse had brought us to the woods when it brought me from the water. These woods were ancient Joan had said, filled with magic.

Grabbing the thyme and holding it next to the bracelet I put both up to my mouth, whispering to it like I had seen Carman do. I asked the faeries to come to our aid and help us banish them, for guidance, and for luck that we safely escape the situation.

Waiting for an answer I quickly thanked the stones, kind of like how with manifestations you're supposed to believe that what you asked for is already yours. Lead with gratitude.

"She can't touch you here," a man's voice said behind us.

Whipping my head around in alarm I pulled a muscle in my side I moved so fast. My heart rate increased exponentially, and it took a while longer than it should have to plateau. Finally, my brain agreed this man was not an immediate threat and told my body to chill out.

He was big, like Declan, with dark hair and dark eyes to Declan's lightness. Dressed normally, he could fit in anywhere but there was something ethereal about his presence. Like if you unfocused your eyes you'd see a glow surrounding him.

And he was handsome. Strong features beautifully arranged, thick auburn hair, thick lashes lining his dark eyes and full lips pulled up in a grin, showing perfect white teeth. My heart picked up again for different reasons.

Trying to regulate my breathing and stop staring at him I chanced a glance at Declan. He didn't look happy. Shit.

"And who are you?" Declan said, accent in full force.

"Ruad Rofhessa," the man said, his deep voice with an accent to match Declan's.

God, but they both oozed masculinity. I was in trouble.

"Okay great and what are you doing here?" Declan said, not sounding thrilled.

"Your bonny lass over here asked for help. I'm here to oblige her," he said winking at me, that handsome smile tilting up just a hair more.

Uh-oh.

"How?" I asked to break their pissing contest.

"Ah well, I'm the man with the plan, the man of knowledge. Here to assist folk like yourselves. The Dál gCais you were once called but I haven't seen your kind in quite some time now."

"Huh?" I all but drooled.

"Mortals with powers of the Tuatha. Your clan was the Dál gCais. We haven't needed you for centuries but Carman and her sons over there have managed to make it back here it seems."

"Back from where? And how can we put her back there?" I asked.

"That's a touch more complicated I'm afraid. She was killed centuries ago," he said.

"Okay...so we have to kill her again? How was it done the first time?"

"That's a story for after we get rid of her now."

"Okay great, so back to my original question of how?" I was getting irritated now, handsome or not.

"Just tell the wee folk for now."

The wee folk, sure, why not?

Taking initiative this time instead of waiting on his reply I whispered to the thyme to make the witch and her sons disappear.

This time instead of thousands of needles pricking at me, a warm sensation spread through me like sunshine. Sort of how you feel when you eat hot soup.

Starting low in my belly and spreading out from me I could feel those tendrils of warmth finding their way into the earth and the trees surrounding me.

Carman and her sons seemed repulsed, backing away and leaving with one last look toward me, resentment on her face.

"Well, that was easy," I said.

Ruad laughed. It was a warm sound, full of life.

"This time sure, but don't let her fool you. It's the woods that did it this time, but she won't quit," he said suddenly sober.

"Don't suppose we could stay in the woods?" Declan chimed in.

"No, I don't suppose so. Now let's go inside so we can talk," Ruad said.

Following Declan to his car, we all clambered in, Sid and the horse following behind. I was a little amazed the horse joined but given the events of late, I suppose I shouldn't have been.

When we got up to the house, I asked the men what we ought to do about him.

"Enbarr will do as he pleases, much like Failinis," Ruad said.

"Who?" I asked.

"Enbarr is the horse, of course, and Failinis is the hound," he answered.

"Of course," I said.

"Come inside and it will all make sense," he said.

Declan led the charge into the house, and I hadn't forgotten that Loretta had placed protection herbs at the door. Checking as discreetly as possible I saw them in place, and I coughed into my elbow as an excuse to see Ruad in my peripheral vision. He walked right in without a flinch. Figuring that was a good sign I felt a little bit more comfortable.

I played host, getting drinks and something to snack on. I

needed a breather more than I wanted to be polite. This day was wearing on me, and I really couldn't wait for it to be over. Plus we hadn't eaten or drank anything in hours.

The kitchen was everything I wanted it to be. Big and bright with a huge fireplace and wood-burning stove. With stainless steel appliances, it was a wonderful marriage between old and new.

Bringing the tray of things I had found into the dining room, Declan and Ruad were essentially having a staring contest. They both looked up at me when I walked in, and I could feel the masculinity in the room.

"So," I said putting the tray down. "Start talking,"

"Right to business, huh? I like that about you," Ruad said with a wink.

Declan cleared his throat, an attempt to take charge of the situation. The ear-splitting grin on Ruad's face told me he enjoyed ruffling Declan's feathers. When neither of us spoke up, Ruad began.

"So we will assume you know about the Tuatha Dé Danann," he said, continuing when we nodded, "and you've met the witch and I assume you have an idea this is not normal?"

We nodded again.

"Right so the beginning I guess. Once, when men and Gods lived together, there was a clan, the Dál gCais. They were favored by the Tuatha for their strength and their nobility, gaining their trust with their loyalty.

"So much so that as thanks for their faithfulness they were gifted with the traits of the Tuatha. Different gifts, and different combinations of gifts would be passed down through their lineage, so long as those individuals possessed the traits so favored by the Tuatha.

"By design or by favor, the lineage did survive, though not everyone born of the clan is gifted. Despite belief, it was not one direct lineage but there were a few clans that gained that favor, all dubbed the same name. They are descendants of the aos sí, the faeries that are in those woods we were just in.

"The faeries are still very real, and they're direct descendants of the Tuatha. The clans are the human equivalent. Those gifted naturally with insight and a touch of magic and who will use that wisely. That's the two of you."

Declan and I exchanged glances. We were sure I had something, but we were dubious that he did.

"Yes, Bridget, your traits have always been a little obvious haven't they? And since you started paying attention to them they're happy to participate. Declan has skills as well but they're not as obvious. The dog, Failinis, has been following Bridget?" he asked.

"Yes, since the day I met her," Declan said.

"Yes because he's your dog."

"Mine?"

"Declan you have the traits of Lugh, savior, warrior, and king. Descended from the Fomorians you have your large stature, but you personify the favorable traits of your Tuatha heritage.

"Failinis is your dog, called invincible in battle and ruler of other animals, he protects his king and queen." He paused after that one, looking first at Declan and then me.

He gave a small smile that seemed a little sad. Gone was the laughter that had been evident in his eyes since we had met him. Recovering quickly he continued.

"Enbarr is yours too, *Lugh*," he said with a smirk. "He can travel land and water. Quicker than any other horse it is said that if you are astride his back, you cannot be killed. Both animals are drawn to the beautiful Bridget, or Brigid because she is the goddess of domesticated animals and your queen."

There was the sadness again.

"Because our Bridget here is the famed Brigid, wise woman, healer, smith, protector, and poet. She is the goddess of domesticated animals and will protect her people with words, healing, or weapons. And as you've seen, her animals can be weapons too,

I didn't miss that he said *our* Bridget.

"Carman and her sons, Darkness, Evil, and Violence, spread their dark deeds throughout Ireland when they were at their prime. Causing famine, death, and destruction, they were finally defeated by the Tuatha. All perishing eventually.

"God of poetry, Ai Mac Ollamain, white sorceress, Bé Chuille, satirist, Cridhinbheal, and magician, Lugh are the ones that led to their demise. All represented here by poet and sorceress, Bridget, and satirist and magician, Declan," he finished with a flourish.

Declan looked angry, but I had to shut my mouth. I was surprised I wasn't drooling, to be honest.

His soliloquy was far-fetched but elaborate, and somewhat believable. Only one question came to mind.

"So are we descended from those other people too?" I asked.

"You're a unique combination of different abilities. Like everyone else is, with the exception that yours and Declan's are especially favorable.

"Years ago when Carman was defeated, the four that vanquished her and her sons created a spell. In essence, the spell was a fail-safe. So long as the Dál gCais survived, they would act as the defenders of the earth.

"In the other realm, there has been *tumult.* I have been trying to determine whether Carman started it or merely benefitted from it. Dark magic has been felt lately and the two of you are proof that such magic is more real than we had hoped.

"My job in both realms is to be the bearer of knowledge. I know our history and our secrets and everything in between. But I do not possess the skills to eradicate Carman and company. That's why we have you," he said in finality.

"And what are we supposed to do?" Declan asked.

"Well, that's up to you. I'll give you what I know that might help you but the two of you are the only ones who can defeat the witches."

"How did they do it the last time?" I asked.

"The sons were handled with what most offended them. Darkness with light, Evil with purity, Violence with kindness. Carman it is said was imprisoned and eventually died of loneliness. How exactly this was accomplished is unclear."

"Of course it is," Declan scoffed with his accent thick.

I was already thinking through possibilities, but I knew who would most likely know the best answers.

"We need to go see your parents again," I said to Declan.

"Right, my mom will most likely know what to do. Seems to me Mr. Knowledge ought to, but he doesn't want to be helpful apparently."

Ruad only had a twinkle in his eye to portray any emotions he had about that statement. I wasn't sure if it was anger or amusement.

"I have given what I can, the rest is up to the two of you. If you need me, call," Ruad said before vanishing from the table.

Everyone was always disappearing.

"Do you think I could disappear?" I asked Declan.

He just stared at me.

"Well everyone else keeps doing it. I think it would be a neat trick,"

"That's what you're leading with?" he asked.

I just shrugged.

"No, Bridget, I don't think it works like that. But then again, what do I know?"

"How do we call him?"

"What?"

"I mean he didn't like give us a phone number or anything. What do I say his name three times like *Beetlejuice*?"

"I don't know. And I don't care. Bridget are you alright?"

"Yeah, I'm pretty sure, you?"

He let out a breath and ran his hands through his hair. Those reddish locks looked like this wasn't the first time today he had done so and suddenly I was very present again. I put my hand on his and squeezed.

"Bridget, I came back here after verbally attacking you for nothing and you were underwater. A magic horse saves you and a God is telling us we're demigods or something here to conquer ancient witches and you're like 'what's his phone number'?"

I laughed.

"Yeah, I'm following you now. I don't know, my brain just kind of compartmentalized all of that already. I guess it's just dealing with it like any other kind of trauma. Tucking it away to be handled at a later date." I had my fair share of chaos in my life; the mind is a powerful thing.

"Bridget, I thought I lost you," he whispered.

"Yeah, I know, I'm sorry," I whispered back.

He grabbed my face in his hands, reminding me of our size difference, and kissing me firmly before pulling me onto his lap in a hug that took my breath away. I didn't mind at all.

Wrapping my arms around his neck I held him to me just as tightly. Well, as tightly as I could manage. His laughter was a low, satisfying rumble that was less humor and more content-ment.

"You're a piece of work, you know that?" he said.

"You wouldn't want me any other way," I said, again quoting the song we loved.

"Okay. Alright. Now that I'm a little more settled, how are you really? And what happened?" he said.

"Well after you lost your shit for no discernible reason…"

"Yeah, I'm sorry about that."

"Bygones."

"I really am sorry. But Evil must have gotten my necklace off while I was distracted with Nick touching you, and Nick easily could have taken yours off.

"My mom helped me deduce that and then she drew the sym-bol on me. So I had driven there and sped back and when I drove up, you were nowhere to be seen but Sid was absolutely mad at the edge of the lake."

"Failinis."

He glared at me.

"Well, that's his name," I muttered.

"Yeah okay, the dog was going mad, and then next thing I know you're coming out of the water like a bat out of hell on some swimming horse."

"Enbarr," I supplied.

"Bridget."

"Well, after I was berated," I lifted an eyebrow at him, "I felt like taking a walk. Thinking the faeries in the woods would hold more answers for me, I asked the thyme for help. About where Failinis was barking is where the thing dragged me underwater.

"It was a male mermaid I guess. Like the selkie. Quick, like seriously fast. I was down at the bottom of the lake in an instant, so I started grabbing the seaweed growing up from the bottom to slow the thing down. It worked. It got mad at me and seemed confused. I don't think I was supposed to be able to talk to him, but the thyme must have allowed me to."

"Bridget, I don't think you were supposed to be conscious at that point, never mind talking to the thing. I must have been gone an hour, there's no telling just how long you were underwater. You came out with the horse halfway across the lake."

"It didn't feel like a long time..."

"Hold your breath for a minute and tell me if it was that long or longer."

When he put it that way, maybe it was longer than I thought. In terms of breath holding ability, anything longer than thirty seconds would be difficult. Then I remembered.

"Aquamarine, your mother gave me aquamarine. I think she meant it for its calming properties, and to release emotional trauma, but she mentioned it protecting sailors from drowning. Maybe that was why I was able to be underwater that long."

"Likely, so what then?" Declan asked.

"Well, after the thing whipped around to ask me how I was talking and conscious I guess, Enbarr was there in an instant and just whirled me away from the thing. Then I was out of the water, and you showed up."

"So we're thinking the mermaid man was what? Violence?"

"Yeah, or more like they can possess things. Or people. And it makes sense that was the third attempt at getting me."

"But not killing you?"

"It doesn't seem so does it? If they wanted me dead, that would have been easy enough. Same as your father. No, I think they want me for something. Maybe that was what was behind the attack on your father. More about exploiting an opportunity to get to me than hurting him."

"It's possible. Ruad mentioned something else happening. Some other dark force. And he doesn't know how they were alive either. Maybe they need you for that and it's connected?"

"That's my train of thought as well. But what if I had drowned in the lake?"

"I think we're beyond the days of the dead staying dead."

"That's not a comforting thought. Do you think whatever that other thing is lives in the lake?"

"I doubt it but it's not outside the realm of possibilities. I would like to take this all to my mom but I'm exhausted and hungry. How about I call them and ask them to come here with pizza?"

"Pizza? Here? No, I'm too spoiled I think for what you call pizza here. I want a Reuben. Do you do that here? Or is that only an American Irish thing?"

"American Irish thing that we've adopted to accommodate you tourists."

"Well, I'll take it. You have terrible food anyway."

"It's not terrible."

"You aren't known for your cuisine. No one says they're in the mood for Irish food. Maybe corned beef and cabbage on Saint Patrick's Day but that's it."

"Because you're such a connoisseur of Irish food."

"I'm just saying."

He smirked and kissed me.

"I will get you the least repugnant food we have then," he said.

As he dialed I put everything away from our small lunch. I was close to dead on my feet after finally resting a while, all of the adrenaline crashing suddenly.

I put the kettle on so we could have some tea and maybe wake up a little before his parents got here. Rummaging through cabinets I found the tea and some mugs.

Declan came and found me before the water was ready. Coming to wrap his arms around my waist he held me close for a moment, neither of us speaking, just savoring the moment.

Pulling back, Declan kissed my temple before disentangling himself completely. I squeezed his hand in appreciation as he did so.

"My parents will be here in an hour or so. My mom has a list of ingredients and books she will be bringing along, and I found you some not gross food," he said, smirking at the last.

"Thanks. I thought we could have some tea before then."

"Yes, I think we should. I could fall asleep here."

"Me too."

The kettle started to whistle, so I set about getting us two mugs of tea. We each took our mug into the living room and Declan started a fire in the hearth.

Outside the light was quickly fading, making the green greener and the shadows darker. It was an eerie feeling knowing that anyone or anything could be looking back at me, and I was completely unaware of it.

Declan joined me on the couch once the fire was blazing, pulling me onto his chest. Leaning my head back onto him, I hugged the arm he had secured around me. If I didn't survive this mess, at least I had known moments like these, I thought.

※　※　※

Declan was softly shaking my shoulder. I must have fallen asleep, still wrapped up in his arms, tea untouched. Night had officially descended, and the only light came from the fire.

"My parents will be here soon," he said softly.

Sitting up and rubbing the sleep from my eyes I grabbed the tea, now cold, and took a large gulp. I hated waking up and having to talk to people so I tried to wake myself up quickly. The tea helped. The caffeine might take a while, but it was cold which helped.

"How long was I out?" I asked.

"Only about a half-hour, forty-five minutes. You didn't last a second once you got comfortable," he said.

"Yeah, seriously," I mumbled.

He ran a hand through my hair. "You needed it. Now drink your tea, maybe do some jumping jacks so you're fully awake when they get here."

Declan knew how grumpy I was when I woke up, not just from lately but from those early morning parties we sometimes worked. The engagement party brunches and early baby showers. Me at work by 9 am was never a good thing.

Focusing on waking up I did get up, walking around the room to turn lights on and stretch. As I did so I remembered part of my dream I had when I slept.

I was alone, walking down the streets of what I guessed was some town in Ireland. A small man had come up to me, drunk and laughing at me. He was inches from my face and his smile showed browned teeth.

The gin blossoms on his face were angry red spider veins that matched what was left of his red hair, thin and spindly as spider legs would be.

I made a face, remembering the dream, shaking my head to clear the image of the man. For some weird reason I thought he was nice, sending me a hello more than anything. I finished to see Declan was staring at me.

"Weird dream," I said.

There was a knock at the door a second later and Declan went to get it. Passing me he kissed me until my toes curled.

"I hope it wasn't about me. Hate to see that look on your face if you were dreaming of me." He laughed.

I smiled "No! At least I hope not. Just keep going to the gym."

"No problem," he said, smacking my butt once before heading to the door.

I followed after him, holding the door open while he took bags from his mother. While the men carried the food to the dining room, I helped his mother out of her coat and hung it in the closet.

"How are you, dear? Declan told us some of what happened," Joan said, hugging me to her.

"I'm alright, thanks to you. If it wasn't for you I don't know what would have happened."

"Nonsense, you would have figured it out."

I was glad for her vote of confidence but truthfully I wasn't so sure. Gracefully accepting the compliment we moved to the dining room to eat dinner.

Declan had gotten me a Reuben as I had asked but in front of him was a shepherd's pie. I smiled at him, and he knew what I meant. He got me there, that was one of my favorite dishes. But still, everything Italian is delicious; you simply can't say the same for Irish fare.

Digging in I let Declan talk for us, explaining in more detail the events that had unfolded during the day. While I listened I couldn't help but think to myself what a day it truly had been. Thinking back on the dream, I wondered if it tied in.

"So you're Lugh are you?" Joan said to Declan when he had finished.

"That's what he said."

"I wonder who that makes us," Joan mused.

"Maybe someone, maybe no one. He made it seem like you may carry some or none of the traits of whatever magical people had gone before us. You could have multiple traits of different people too."

"Now, what do we do?" Joan asked.

"We were hoping you would have the answer to that," Declan answered.

"Sorry, love. Nothing comes to mind at the moment, but I brought my best books and trinkets. I think we should start with looking up the mythology online. Specifically, yourselves first. Make a list of your strengths, weaknesses, and any weapons you might have had according to the myth. I think that would be most useful. And a bit about this Ruad character. You can't be too sure,"

We agreed so after finishing dinner and cleaning up we settled in the living room to research. Splitting assignments I ended up with myself and Carman. It made sense since we were foes.

Before I could focus on myself though I had to check out Ruad. From what little there was, it seemed to me that he was who he said he was. Associated with ravens for their intelligence, it got me thinking about the multiple ravens I saw before all of this.

Maybe Ruad had eyes on me for a while already. I wonder what he saw...

I had already researched Brigid, but I pored through more to see what else jumped out at me. Brigid the healer, the smith, the protector. Nothing was jumping out at me.

Switching to Carman there wasn't much there either. I guess that's what happens in thousands of years of history. There wasn't anything outlined in neon and written in all caps with instructions on how to defeat her.

What it did say was that Lugh, Bé Chuille, Ai Mac Ollamain, and Cridhinbheal were the ones to do it. Looking into each individually, Lugh was indeed the owner of both Failinis and Enbarr.

He was king, warrior and savior. Associated with truth, law, and oaths. Having numerous weapons, counting Failinis and Enbarr, he also had a fiery spear and a sling stone. Which I assumed was a slingshot.

Interesting to me was that he was grandson to a Fomorian, the mean giants of the lore. But more interesting that it said here his son was a hero named Cú Chullain.

The Hound of Chullain was a formidable warrior in service to Chullain after killing the chieftain's hound. Sometimes he is described as human and sometimes more like a God.

It got me thinking though that Lugh had so many weapons...

"Declan, were you ever any good with a slingshot? Or a spear maybe?" I asked.

"Not that I'm aware of."

"It just says here that you had weapons and you have two of the four here. Maybe we need to find the other two?"

"Or make the other two, smith?"

"I would more than likely burn myself or the building I was in instead of making a spear, but it's a thought I guess."

"I've heard something about a spear," Brian chimed in. "At the golf course. There's a legend that there is an abandoned building haunted by an old drunkard. Says there's an enchanted weapon, spear if I'm remembering correctly, that was forged by the fires of hell.

"When you're in the woods looking for your ball, you might happen upon the spirit of the old man. Once you meet him they say you won't find your ball or your marbles again if you catch my drift."

"Is that the woods that the witch got to you?" Joan asked Brian.

"The very same. Only I hear you have to be a really bad shot to find the abandoned house."

"It's worth a shot to go look there if you ask me," Joan said.

"Anything about a slingshot?" I asked.

"No, but that's easy enough to make," Brian answered.

"Has anyone got anything else?" Declan asked.

It was a collective 'no.' How would we know what to look for? The weapon may be important but in truth who knew?

Brigid didn't have any weapons, maybe her wit. Brigantia, which was the English version didn't either. I had never worked a forge in my life, but Brigid was good at it. Maybe I had to make a weapon. I really hoped not.

After another half hour or so we called it quits only really distinguishing that Declan was the man with the weapons, apparently. Rustling up some dessert from the kitchen and deciding we would go tomorrow to the golf course to see what we could find, we said good night to his parents.

As we walked them out, I scanned the dark woods to find Ruad there in the darkness. I guess that was a comfort. He winked at me, and I pretended not to be affected. Damn it.

Watching them leave from the front door I stifled a yawn. Now that the day was through I was having trouble keeping my eyes open. It didn't pass Declan's observance which was evident by how he picked me up and carried me up the stairs after he locked up.

"That's really unnecessary you know," I said as I snuggled in closer.

"Taking care of you will never be unnecessary."

"I can take care of myself," I huffed.

"I know but I can do it better," he rumbled.

Without much to say to that, I kissed his chest. He's done a pretty good job so far at least. Once he laid me on the bed he started undressing me and I was suddenly very awake.

# CHAPTER 10

Waking up early after staying up far later than planned I was in a better mood than I should have been. A night with Declan will do that to a girl. Blushing even as I thought it I looked at him sheepishly.

I was grateful he was preoccupied with a map he had found of the golf course. He was looking to see the best point of entry to the deepest part of the woods so we could be as quick as possible. When he did things like that it was easy to picture him as a CEO of a billion-dollar business.

The intensity in his gaze was palpable, like a lion on the hunt. His shoulders were tense like they were ready to pounce. But he was calm. The type of calm that only the best predators are capable of.

*I wonder what that makes me,* I thought. Was I prey? Or a fellow predator? The smile on my face made me think predator.

"Find anything yet?" I asked as I grabbed my coffee.

"Right over here," he said as he pointed to a spot on the map.

I got up and walked behind him, an excuse to be near him. My feelings for him grew at an alarming rate, already feeling very possessive. For some reason, it didn't scare me as much as it had. And that should scare me.

He was pointing at a spot near one of the holes on the course, seven I think, but his huge hand obstructed my view. The woods were situated on the right-hand side of most of the course. The course was a wavy rectangle. Beyond the tree line were woods for miles until they butted up to farmland.

It was beautiful and I could imagine hunting in there with my father. His hunting club near Declan's home in New Jersey was similar, farmland and woods for miles for the deer and pheasant to roam freely. Until they weren't so free anymore.

Many people think it's cruel to hunt but eat chicken from the supermarket. Like the chicken raised in a building, never seeing the light of day, is somehow better for the animal. Or the cow packed two hundred deep in the muck without the freedom to roam.

I think hunting is the best way to honor the animal. It takes guts to kill something yourself. Whenever my father did, I would silently thank the animal for its sacrifice to feed us as Native Americans did.

The rumor of the old man of the woods and the ancient building hiding in there made sense. I could imagine many farmers, hunters, and golfers alike wandering in there. That was probably why it wasn't developed as so much around it was.

"Alright so how do we access it? Play a few rounds until we get to that hole?" I asked.

"That or we could try to walk the length of the woods, but the parking lot and the main building don't skirt the woods. We would have to try to act nonchalant through a lot of open land before we hit the woods and hike through them. I think with playing a few rounds of golf we may be able to just drive the cart off into the woods, save time."

"I like the sound of that better. What time does it open?"

"In an hour, so we should hurry. I'll leave a message for Loretta, and we can grab something quick to eat on the way there. You shower and I'll make us two coffees to go," he said, standing and kissing my forehead.

He was so much trouble.

In the bathroom I was busy thinking of the day ahead of us when someone cleared their throat behind me. Dressed in only a bra and underwear I turned to see Ruad standing there, leaning against the door jamb with arms and feet crossed openly staring at me.

"What the hell are you doing here?" I said, crossing my arms before realizing that wasn't helping anything.

Ruad noticed and smirked.

"Just came to remind you that you're the healer."

"Great, thanks. Is that all?" I answered back, voice dripping with sarcasm.

"I'd be lying if I didn't mention I came to enjoy the view."

"Have you had your fill then?" I said with a vehemence I only half felt.

"Not even a little bit," he answered with a wink before disappearing.

"Great, more trouble," I grumbled as I double-checked he wasn't naked behind the curtain or something before getting into the shower myself.

What the hell was that all about? I was torn between thinking he genuinely was trying to be helpful or just trying to see me undressed.

It was a little odd that he was so...flirtatious. But then, what did I know about Gods or whatever he was?

What I did know was he was unbelievably handsome in a way that clashed with Declan. Declan was fierce and serious to Ruad's playful lightness. If it weren't for the measures we had taken to evil proof the house I'd think Ruad very suspect.

Though I would be remiss not to mention both men's obvious dominance. They can be playful, but they weren't house cats.

As it was though, the salt lined the window in here and the rue, mugwort, and yarrow were there when I passed the door last. Maybe being centuries-old just gave him a different view of things. The God of knowledge you would think would be world weary. Instead, he was jovial and mischievous, so far.

There was something about him I couldn't get over. When he did these things like popping up in the bathroom or keeping watch over us from the tree line, I felt like a gravitational pull to him. I wanted to be near him for reasons that had nothing to do with his good looks.

I felt that way about Declan too.

With Declan, I had thought it was more about my vulnerability at that point in my life. Just ending my shit show of a relationship with Nick, the blowout with friends and family, and my recent sobriety.

It was no wonder I couldn't get enough of Declan. He was everything good in the world, right after some of the worst in the world. Like sunshine after a long winter, I had needed him like I had needed few things before.

But Ruad was different. As it was, I still knew very little about him. And I was in a great place in my life. Declan filled every ache I had previously.

So why such a pull?

Just like with Declan, I felt my body yearn for his presence. For the peace and happiness I knew was there. Like a sunflower drawn to the sun, I wanted to follow both men all of my days. Except I couldn't.

Stepping out of the shower with no more knowledge than when I went in I hurried through the rest of getting ready. Throwing on jeans, boots, and a flannel with a long sleeve shirt underneath I felt like myself. There was no better outfit in my opinion.

The only part I felt uncomfortable about was telling Declan that Ruad had popped up in the bathroom as I was undressing. I didn't think that would go over well. But I also thought that not telling him wouldn't go over well either.

As I turned to head out the door, Declan was there watching me.

"What's wrong?" he said. His brows were furrowed, and I thought again of the vast difference in demeanor between him and Ruad.

Damn it. I wasn't ready.

"Ruad told me to remember I was the healer." There, that was easy enough.

"In the shower?"

Damn.

"In the bathroom..." I said on a sigh. "I was in my bra and underwear, so it wasn't that bad."

"Not that bad? And was he there when you got undressed?"

"Well, I don't know how long he was there. He wasn't there when I went in, but he was there when I was mostly undressed and then he was gone before I showered. I made sure."

"Are you all right?"

I wasn't expecting that.

"Yeah, I mean it's the equivalent of if I was wearing a bikini. He did mention it wasn't an accident, but he doesn't seem harmful to me, flirtatious at worst."

"I agree. I'm not happy but that's a conversation for him, not you."

"What?" I said, a little taken aback.

"Were you expecting me to blame you?"

"Kinda."

"Did you ask him to join you in the bathroom?"

"Well, no."

"And you told me the truth?"

"Yeah."

"So why would I be mad at you?" he said with a laugh.

Shaking his head, he came over and kissed me thoroughly.

"Are you still mine?" he whispered.

"I suppose so," I whispered back.

"Mmm, suppose so? Should I prove it to you?" he said, lifting me by my hips and wrapping my legs around his waist. Pushing me against the wall he leaned in to kiss me gently, moving to kiss my neck to continue his assault of my senses. His hands were firmly on my hips, and I arched into him, seeking more.

"You're mine," he said with a growl as he lowered me to the ground, "and your undergarments are much sexier than a bikini."

Smacking my ass, he went off to the shower without another word, leaving me breathless. I was in so much trouble. And the damn man knew it too.

Shaking my head as I walked down the hall I remarked on our relationship a month ago as opposed to now. A month ago I didn't even imagine what it would be like kissing Declan. Now I couldn't get kissing him out of my head.

Fighting the urge to go join him in the shower I wandered into the kitchen to put together some snacks to take with us. I always liked to be prepared for anything. The coffees he had made were on the counter and by the time I threw together a few snacks he was done with his shower.

Joining me in the kitchen with his normally vibrant hair dulled from being wet, perfectly tousled, I had to fight the urge to undress him all over again.

Taking a deep breath I took one last long look at his black thermal stretched deliciously across his broad chest, knowing those tattoos underneath were begging me to explore them more.

The forest green flannel he wore loosely over the top of his shirt barely hid the muscles underneath, making his green eyes shine like emeralds even from this distance.

"Uh, I got some snacks," I said, averting my eyes as I stumbled on the words a little.

Deep breaths, Bridget.

His deep chuckle sent a thrill through me as he crossed the room to stand behind me. Putting a hand on my hip he pulled my hair away from my neck and kissed me lightly at the base of it. Goosebumps erupted all over and I arched into him again.

"Later," he promised.

Incapable of coherent words I groaned in response. This was always the fun of a new relationship, wasn't it? The can't keep your hands off each other phase. I hoped it would never end.

With Declan, that is.

Sobering a little at my thoughts I tried to quiet the alarm bells that rang out that this was only temporary. Would we tire of each other when the adventure was over? Or would I screw it up?

Trying to ignore the idea of this flame fizzling out I stared at Declan's departing, hulking, figure. Hard to imagine I would tire of him.

Easy to imagine I would self-sabotage.

Ruad came to mind. He was a likely candidate.

Try as I might, I couldn't ignore the attraction I had for him. The difference mainly being that he wasn't human, and curiosity killed the cat.

Even my self-sabotaging tendencies wouldn't go that far, right?

Damn it. I was already doing it and I knew it. His not being human was precisely why he was even more attractive to me. My imagination was already getting the best of me...

So I was screwed up? At least I knew I was and tried to save me from myself.

Declan was too important to me. Which was both a blessing and a curse.

My family was proof that it's the people closest to you that had the power to destroy you.

And they exercised that power ruthlessly.

"Where did you go, Bridget?" Declan asked.

Swallowing the rage that had already spiked my adrenaline, I answered evenly and calmly. Hiding emotions was usually my forte.

Somehow Declan always knew.

"I'm fine, just preparing for the day ahead of us," I said.

"That's not true and you know it. You went all frosty there for a second."

"Frosty?"

"You're a regular ice queen when you want to be."

"Hmm. Just went off on a tangent. I'm fine."

Putting his coffee and the bag we had packed with things we might need in the car he took mine out of my hands and did the same.

Grabbing my face with both big hands he stared into my eyes. I felt the ice melt and so did he.

"You can tell me when you're ready, Bridget. You know I wouldn't hurt you."

Did I though? Family wasn't supposed to hurt you and yet they did it all the time. Like it was a sport.

Taking a deep breath I didn't know I needed I felt the knot

that had formed in my chest loosen. He knew how to speak to the heart of me.

Kissing me slowly I felt the rest of the tension bleed from my muscles until I was putty.

"Okay," I breathed into him before pulling him in for one more kiss.

Maybe he wouldn't hurt me. I just hoped I wouldn't hurt him either.

That's the catch. I was always so ready to be hurt I did the hurting before they could. But I couldn't do that with Declan; he was too important.

Failinis and Enbarr had joined us outside, emerging from whatever shadows they retreated to when we weren't together. They were both waiting expectantly for us.

"Sorry folks, we can't bring you with us today," Declan said to the pair.

They continued to look at us but neither acknowledged his words. It was true, we couldn't bring them golfing with us, but it wasn't something I was happy about. In truth, I felt naked going there without them.

I gave each a pat and a hug and told them to be good. Probably a fruitless gesture but I was feeling awfully attached to them too lately. And animals never did me wrong so I could love them, and them me, unabashedly.

We got in the car, and I waved goodbye to them, still stoic watching us depart. Declan squeezed my hand, and I gave him a small smile. Truthfully I was a little nervous about today, having ignored it until I couldn't anymore. I just didn't know what to expect.

❖ ❖ ❖

It was a quiet ride as both of us were preoccupied with our thoughts. It seemed to me that we arrived much quicker than we probably actually had. But it was also early and I'm not a morning person. For all I knew I fell asleep for a while.

We made it just as the doors opened, which was the plan. Making our way inside Declan did all the talking, and I merely nodded and smiled. Buttoning up and tucking in our plaid shirts we looked only a little out of place. But I wasn't about to hike through the woods in golf gear.

Trading in our boots we put on golf shoes but tucked our boots into a backpack to take with us. I felt terribly unprepared. Our plan felt ludicrous now that we were here. Just walk around aimlessly in the woods? There was probably a tracker on the golf cart. We might not even make it that far.

Too little too late at this point. I had a knife that my dad had bought me tucked into the waistband of my pants and that was it weapon wise. Unless Declan had something too.

Either way we knew too little about this spirit or faerie we were about to meet. Too little about ourselves in this new magical world. And not nearly enough about Ruad.

I trusted Failinis and Enbarr. Beyond just that they were animals, both had proven to be trustworthy. Ruad could be knowingly sending us on a fool's errand with false information for all we knew.

I know he wasn't the one to tell us about the haunted woods, but he knew what we were doing today. As evidenced by my visit in the bathroom today.

It was making me a little nervous to think of how much he really did know and maybe wasn't telling us. He could be leading us to our deaths.

Clubs and bags in the cart we hopped in and headed to the first hole. Silly me was also nervous because I had never golfed before. Declan knew this but for some reason I didn't want to look like a fool in front of him.

Stopping to tee up I looked to see Declan grinning from ear to ear. His green eyes were alight with that mischief I loved so much. His reddish hair curled out from under a ball cap, and he looked so young and carefree that for a second I felt like I was seeing him for the first time.

"What?" I said to him.

"I'm excited to golf with you. We might as well have some fun before heading into God knows what."

"I've never golfed before." I groaned.

"That's the fun, I get to teach you," he said with a wink.

He hopped out of the cart and went about getting us ready, explaining all the while. I mostly kept up with what he was saying but I was more interested in watching him. Every muscle was on display as he moved around, full of boyish energy I wasn't used to seeing.

While he was often mischievous, he wasn't often carefree. That was what I loved most about him, he could surprise me. Each day a new layer was unveiled, and each day I found that I loved all of them.

Grabbing my hand he hauled me out of the cart and towards where he had set us up, golf club in the other hand. Pulling me tightly against him, my back to his front, I couldn't help the smile that overtook me. I really liked this side of him.

Placing the club in my hands he adjusted my hands with his own. Grabbing each of my legs in turn he adjusted my stance and my hips until he was satisfied. I was satisfied to just be in his arms.

"Alright now you're going to raise your arms up and then swing, putting your weight behind the swing. Do you have any questions?" he said.

"Will you do this one with me?" I asked. I could do it myself, but I wanted to savor his embrace as long as possible.

"My pleasure," he said, letting go with one hand to wrap his arm around my waist and kiss the top of my head.

Truthfully, I was amazed he could shrink down to help me, being so much larger than I was. But man it felt good to do something normal like go on a date with Declan. Even if it wasn't a date, I was determined to savor this moment of lightheartedness and treat it like one.

He got back into position and as he swung up, I felt every delicious muscle of his move with me. The downswing was equally delectable, and I was genuinely surprised at how far the ball went, thinking I would be a hindrance in his swing. I thought wrong.

"Get it now?" he asked.

"Mmm," was all I could say, melting into him further.

"You're insatiable." He laughed, and the deep timbre of his voice rumbled in my chest we were so close.

"It's nice. A little normalcy."

"I know," he whispered as he squeezed me tighter. "Now move, it's my turn."

Chuckling, I stepped aside. His swing was a sight to be seen, and the ball was not. It sailed away farther and faster than I thought possible, and I marveled at him again, wishing this could last a while longer.

The rest went by much quicker than I was hoping that it would. It was empty on the course with the exception of staff. That was the advantage of an early weekday. Declan checked the map before the seventh hole so we could see what the landscape was like.

There was a curve before you got to the hole that was where we would enter the woods. From our vantage point, we could see it up ahead. Nerves started to snake their way through my insides, making me tense.

Declan grabbed my hand, and I looked at him. Gone was the lightness that had danced across his features earlier and in its place was the serious scowl I was more used to. I gave him a small smile.

"Ready?" I said.

"As ever," he answered.

Leaning in he kissed me, just a peck but the meaning was there. What he didn't say was, "here goes nothing, if something goes wrong it's been fun."

It had been a lot of fun indeed.

He drove straight to the woods and as we went, I asked the faeries for help, whatever Gods and Goddesses of the forest to keep us safe, and for Enbarr and Failinis to whisk us away if need be.

I also told Ruad to be helpful if he can. No politeness necessary after this morning. And I added in that he should send whatever reinforcements necessary.

I was most nervous because I didn't know what to expect. While I didn't think something would go wrong, I wasn't sold on it. Every shadow I thought was Darkness and every time the wind took the branches I saw Carman's hair.

This besotted faerie, whatever he was, didn't scare me as much. How scary was an old drunk man? I might be able to poke his belly and he would trip over his feet in a drunken stupor.

Mainly I felt miserably unprepared. No weapon to wield with magical powers, no potion to throw at him. Just my brain and my intuition. I wish I trusted myself more.

Suddenly I was ripped from the cart, landing hard on the ground. The impact had blurred my vision and left me a little breathless, but I pulled the knife from my waist, happy to have something.

The cart stopped only a few feet away from me, but Violence was on top of me quicker. Squeezing my neck, keeping the air from reaching my already breathless lungs, his face was twisted in rage. Using the knife I drove it hard and fast into the space I knew to be weakest in defense and what I could reach, under his arm.

I tried to think of him like a deer. So many times growing up I would be deer hunting with my father. Aim right behind the front leg, under the shoulder blade, in the space behind the breastplate and above the ribcage.

As I did, I said a silent prayer to whoever was listening that he stayed dead. I didn't think ancient witches would die just from being stabbed.

I don't know if it was my imagination or if I was fading but I think I saw shock register on his face before he squeezed tighter, putting his weight behind it. Then suddenly he was gone, thrown off of me with force.

I was dimly proud I'd managed to hold on to the knife. It was slick with blood, but it had served me well.

Declan's face swam in front of mine for a second and I nodded at him. I was fine, scared, shook up, but I didn't think anything was lasting. Well maybe the killing part would stick but that wasn't a pressing concern.

Violence flashed back into my vision and some of the fog faded, adrenaline spiking. He tackled Declan, raising a golf club in one hand. He meant to bash Declan over the head with it.

I don't know how but Declan threw him off of him, Violence landed against a tree with a thwack sure to attract attention if anyone was near. We weren't that deep in the woods yet and I was suddenly nervous we would be discovered. What the hell would we say?

There was ivy growing along the length of the tree he had landed against, and I asked it to grow around him. Why not?

As I stared in astonishment, the ivy started to glow with those firefly-looking things from the night I helped Brian. It morphed and moved and wrapped around his torso as he was recovering.

Violence started thrashing and cursing, pulling at the ivy. I asked it to silence him, and it grew right over his mouth.

This was only a temporary solution though. Looking around, I asked any faerie to give me something to permanently subdue him.

That's when the mushrooms caught my eye. They were near the base of a tree, with a little cup-like thing at their base. Going with intuition I was guessing the faeries meant these.

Running over I grabbed a handful, careful to use my sleeve instead of just touching them. Placing some in my flannel shirt pocket for later, I took the biggest one back to Violence.

The ivy had bound him further and there was little of him not covered in the leaves. I asked it to open his mouth, and the ivy parted but I had to get closer to wrench his mouth open.

It took a few tries and eventually, Declan came to assist me, landing one vicious blow to his jaw before grabbing his lower jaw and forehead forcing his mouth to remain open. Glancing at

Declan he nodded once without returning my look and I took it to mean what I knew it meant. Just do it.

Praying this would at least be a clean death I shoved the mushroom into his mouth and Declan closed it immediately. I asked the ivy to hold his mouth shut, and it started to grow right around Declan's hands before he moved them.

Violence held onto his ire all the while, glaring at us, and silently swearing our demise with his hostile gaze. I stared right back.

I was suddenly reminded of *The Game of Thrones*. One of the characters I loved the most, Ned Stark, said that when you ordered the death of a man, you owed it to him to swing the sword. And you can't look away.

I agreed with that. It was honorable and respectful of the act of death itself, if not the man.

Declan watched on with me, placing a big hand on my shoulder as we watched the light fade from Violence's eyes. Almost immediately, the forest floor came up to swallow him.

Death brought new life, and moss, ferns, and other different vegetation took the place of the witch that had just been there. It was beautiful in a way.

End Violence with kindness. Stabbing him wasn't the way, but the mushroom proved to be a peaceful death. A kind one, allowing beauty where there was none previously.

The scuffle was minor, and for that I was grateful. That and the evidence was quickly swallowed up. But it meant that Carman knew we were here, and she didn't like it.

Some far-off part of my brain told me I should be more upset about having just killed someone. Looking at my hand, the knife was still clutched in my fist, but what was blood was now mud.

Declan followed my line of sight and made a noise. He was just as nonplussed.

"I guess it's like we picked a flower more than killed a man," he said.

"Yeah, I can live with it I think."

He made another sound and crossed himself, like a good

Catholic. I followed suit and mumbled something about him resting in eternal peace. A lot of emphasis on eternal.

Getting back into the cart I took a long look at our surroundings. The woods were quiet, so quiet it was unsettling.

Tamping down the fear that rose in my throat I sat in the cart and grabbed Declan's hand a moment for a squeeze of reassurance. Grateful we were in this together.

Continuing on into the woods the foliage got denser the deeper we went. I was watching for Darkness though I knew it was a futile gesture.

There wasn't a building to be seen yet, and I was getting a little over it to be honest. It was feeling less like *Lord of the Rings* and more like the *Twilight Zone* and Rod Serling was about to pop up on the screen.

I could hear his voice in my head. "Bridget and Declan are on a quest that will never end here in the *Twilight Zone*."

Or something like that.

In all sincerity, I did wonder just how true that was. It was only a week or more since this all started. What day was it that I went to Declan's house? What day was today?

"What day is it?" I asked Declan.

There was a long pause.

"Hell if I know, love. Why?"

"Just feels very *Twilight Zone*."

"That sci-fi show?"

"Don't refer to it that way. It's genius."

"Didn't say it wasn't. But it is that sci-fi show."

I harrumphed. I was exhausted and maybe a little delirious suddenly. The weight of the world felt like it was on my shoulders, and I decided closing my eyes was a good idea.

I dreamt I was falling. Those terrible ones where you keep falling and falling with no end in sight.

"Bridget!!!" Declan's voice penetrated my dream.

But I didn't wake up. That wasn't right.

Was I still dreaming?

The landscape changed and instead of falling I was stuck in

that horrible can't wake up space. I tried screaming and nothing happened.

I was still in the woods, but I was alone. Shadows descended all around me so much so that it was difficult to see. Reaching out for the tree nearest me I grasped only air.

These kinds of dreams always freaked me out. My heart rate was accelerating, and I tried screaming again but as loud as I intended it to be there was nothing.

Distantly, I heard Declan calling my name again. I tried running towards him but as much as I moved I stayed in place.

Another voice rang out. Quietly and softly but it was there.

"Stop," it said.

I looked all around but I couldn't see the source. Something was snaking up my back. Touching my back and looking at my hands I noticed they were turning black.

I couldn't feel anything on my back but now my hands were going numb. The black crisscrossed my hands like the veins underneath, snaking up my arms like poison.

"You should have stopped," the voice said again.

I guess this was Darkness. Did he poison me somehow? Stop what?

"Stop what?" I asked him.

An enraged roar echoed through the dream space.

"This path. End this foolishness now. You don't know what you're after, woman," he spat.

The numbness continued to spread up my arms, and I began to shiver.

"What's it to you?" I felt like talking was the right thing to do.

"There is much you don't know."

"Then tell me."

Everything went pitch black, and I felt the panic bubble up my throat. Squelching the fear I tried to focus on what I could sense.

I couldn't see anything at all now. Waving my hand in front of my face didn't work because my hands were numb. Or it did work, and I couldn't see them or feel them. Briefly, I wondered if this was what death was.

Ignoring that thought I refocused again. No sense of smell. Nothing I could touch. I tried to scream again, but either nothing came out or I couldn't hear anything.

Or both. Stupidly I put my tongue out thinking maybe I could taste something.

I'm not even sure it worked. I was robbed of all of my senses, either numb or otherwise, and I had to stop the panic before it took over.

Maybe this was life after death, a nothingness void to be stuck in for an eternity. It was oddly satisfying.

I would almost be content if it weren't for the nagging sense that I wasn't alone. That sixth sense was only heightened by the absence of my other senses until it consumed me. There were many other things that I could sense when I focused.

Anger, loneliness, and a touch of insanity surrounded me. Whatever I was picking up on was restless and irritable. Its emotional volatility left me feeling like I was in the middle of a very deep and dark ocean, tossed about by the waves.

A face suddenly appeared, red and puffy with fire red hair on his head and a beard that matched. His clothes were tattered and clearly from a different century and he smelled like a distillery. And I remembered him from my dream.

Blinking in confusion I rubbed my eyes to clear my head, only to realize I could do that now. Declan's face popped into my view, and I sent him a questioning look.

"You were out. Like not asleep, not dead, not *here* for a while. I shook you a lot and screamed at you and nothing. Then he showed up, and that's where we're at," Declan answered only slightly shaken.

Us getting used to the oddness caused me a moment of worry but I couldn't afford to think of that right now.

"Aye, here I am at last," the man muttered.

Slurred more like.

He sat down and out of my face. Finally I could recognize that he wasn't exactly a man.

"Are you a leprechaun?" I asked.

He muttered a string of entirely unintelligible words. He punctuated with his arms frequently and I continued to stare entranced. Some drool fell out of my mouth as I tried to pick up a word at all and I quickly wiped it away.

"Um, so I think that was a yes?" I said.

I mean from his gestures that's what I picked up.

"Aye, close enough," he said.

Declan started laughing. Laughing!

"What the fuck is wrong with you?" I said as a hysterical giggle escaped my lips.

Before long me and Declan were doubled over in laughter as the leprechaun stared at us with a face I imagine I just had. Which sent Declan and me into further hysteria as we both pointed at the poor man's face as he tried to figure out what was wrong with us.

"That's what you just looked like," Declan said in between breaths. "You even drooled!"

And we lost it again. Because I had. And I did.

After a few more moments of desperately trying to stop our laughter and catch our breath, we finally did. Taking deep breaths we exchanged a concerned but amused look. We both knew we were losing it a little.

"Finished have ye?" the little man said.

"For now," I said.

"What was that?" Declan asked the man.

"You tell me," he answered in a brogue thicker than mashed potatoes.

"I think he meant my, uh, episode. Thank you for getting me out of that by the way. What's your name?" I said to him.

"Darkness got you. Haven't seen him around in a while. Lucky I was in the neighborhood, ye are. Call me Senan. And it's clurichaun not leprechaun," he said.

I was starting to get the hang of his speech. Mostly. I stifled a giggle and tried to sober myself some more. Breathe in, breathe out, do not insult him with laughter.

"That was Darkness? What did he do to me?" I asked.

"Well he would've drowned ye in darkness if he could have," he answered.

"But how? How did you get me out?"

"He poisons you in a manner of speaking. Tricks you into following him into that space between here and there. Then once you're there, you can't find your way out because you can't do much of anything. I just used my magic and popped in to say hello."

"Thank you, again. What's 'there'? And how come you can just pop over there?"

"Nosy, nosy," he said.

"I didn't mean any offense. I just want to figure it all out and I would be happy if you could help me."

"Bonny lass you have here," he said to Declan. "Sweet too. Smart man. Alright, I'll help where I can. 'There' is the spirit world. Where folks go when they're not 'here' anymore. And I can pop anywhere because I'm already of the spirit world. Does that satisfy you?"

I laughed. He was a pip.

"Almost. Can Darkness take me like that again? How do I stop him?"

"With light."

"What does that even mean?" Declan said.

"Oi, she'll know."

I rolled my eyes. This was annoying.

As I did so I caught a glimpse of what I thought were buildings. Whipping my head back to Senan he blanched and poof he was gone.

"What now?" Declan said.

Gone were the buildings, but I had seen them. Sobering a little I remembered why we were here. Senan was guarding the weapons we needed to defeat Carman. Why had he been so helpful though?

"I saw where we need to go. Only, how we are going to get there is the problem."

"That's why he disappeared?"

"I suppose so. He was fairly helpful though, don't you think?"

"That's the way of these folks. They help with one hand and hurt with the other. I think he's afraid."

"Of who? You?"

"Well, now, don't sound so incredulous, my love. Most people are intimidated by me. But most people aren't you.

"No, I mean he's in a precarious position. Help us to defeat Carman and if we fail, she will do very terrible things to him. If we win he may face ridicule of others of his kind. He has to 'allow' us to steal the weapon without actually helping."

"Okay, well, I get that I guess. The spear is near here that much I know,"

I thought of what Joan had given me. Checking out my bracelet I repeated her words in my head. *Emerald for guidance, heliodor for magic and manifestation, serpentine for the luck of the Irish.*

Saying a little prayer that felt right I asked each stone in turn for their help. Opening my eyes, I looked at Declan and let out a whoosh of air I didn't realize I had been holding.

"So?" Declan prompted.

"I asked the crystals for help,"

"Did they answer?"

"Not that I'm aware of."

"So then what do you suppose we do?"

"Well I saw buildings when I rolled my eyes and this is where Senan found us, so I don't want to wander too far."

I rolled my eyes again. Nothing.

"Nope, that didn't work."

I tried closing my eyes. Not sure what I was trying to accomplish but nothing happened.

Walking over to a big rock I peeked under it. Still nothing.

"What are you doing?" Declan asked.

"I don't know, maybe he disappeared down a rabbit hole like *Alice in Wonderland.*"

He just gave me a blank stare.

"Well, you're not coming up with anything groundbreaking."

"Let's just pause a moment. Eat something we packed and relax a little. We can brainstorm or wait for some sign."

"Yeah, okay."

We crawled back into the golf cart, and each took some food and drank some water. Truth be told I was fairly exhausted now that I had a moment, and I was glad for his suggestion. But if we didn't get the spear today, we would only have to do it again.

As I ate, I thought about what Ruad could have possibly meant by me being the healer. How was it applicable here? The only affliction was Senan being a drunk, but that wasn't something you just fixed. I should know.

I was staring off into space as I thought when something caught my eye. Just a movement in a tree. Focusing my attention in the area I saw the disturbance, and a big white face became apparent.

A large barn owl was perched in his hole in a tree maybe one hundred feet away. Shouldn't he be asleep?

"There," I said, knocking Declan with my elbow and pointing with the other hand. "The owl."

"What about it?"

"Let's find out."

Packing up we headed out to where the owl was perched in his tree. He watched our progress unflinchingly, his serene disposition reminding me of his association with wisdom.

It reminded me of my grandmother. My father's mother was stern and stoic and never failed to intimidate me as a child. As an adult I still didn't know how to talk to her, but I was no longer intimidated by her at least.

I wondered if that meant I was become intimidating myself.

Usually I consider myself to have a sweet disposition. But I've been called cold enough times that I guess I'm not as sweet as I think I am. I'm still sweet but maybe a little more standoffish than I realize. And I make it clear I'm not someone to fuck with.

That's the problem. Too sweet you get stepped on. Not sweet enough you're cold. Oh well.

Maybe that was why I couldn't stand nice guys, because I

dominated them. At least with not-nice guys we were evenly matched in dominance.

The owl seemed unconcerned about whether or not I thought he was a nice owl. Which is the way it ought to be.

As we got closer to the tree, I started trying to see the buildings I'd seen earlier. They were old stone with thatched roofs, but I couldn't see anything.

I'm the healer. What the fuck did that mean anyway? Ruad's words came back to me as I stared at more woods with no more idea on what to do from here.

Taking a step forward, nothing happened. I was testing to see if I would be magically transported to the buildings I had seen. No such luck.

Scanning the area I looked up, down, all around and I couldn't find anything obvious. I looked to the owl for some guidance, and he just sat there stoically staring back at me.

Something was discomforting about his level of comfortability with our presence. He should have taken flight or tucked away into his home by now.

His tree was dead and hollow, one of only a few in the area. Clearly ancient, I guess the tree had just had a nice long life and finished his time here on this planet.

Placing a hand on the tree I felt its warmth. Not that the tree was warm, but its energy. That feeling you get when you're stressed and you take a walk in the woods, how that calming energy soothes you. That's where nature baths come from.

That feeling told me the tree wasn't as dead as I thought it was. Well here's a little luck.

Focusing all of my attention on the tree I just listened to what it wanted to tell me. It felt weary. I listened, and I sympathized with it. Weary was an old friend of mine too.

Opening my eyes, I saw it then. All of it. It was a little village with its dirt path for street and stone houses with thatched roofs.

The tree gave a little jolt. Not like a shock but as if it was happy. All living things talk if you bother to listen.

Giving the tree a pat of approval I looked to Declan to see if he saw it too. Except I didn't see Declan.

Shit.

I glanced around the tree.

Nothing.

Called his name.

Nope.

The cart was gone too. Well, hell.

Checking out the tree I saw it was hale and hearty, a sign that I somehow made it and Declan didn't. Maybe I should have been holding his hand or something.

After another few minutes of looking, time was wasting, and for lack of anything better to do I started off to explore. I didn't see anyone or hear anyone. Just me and the woods. And the owl. Still, I set out cautiously, keeping my eyes peeled.

There was no signage that was obvious anywhere. Just a deserted little village. Secretly I was jumping with joy.

I always wanted to live in medieval times. On further contemplation, I was unsure whether I had entered a different realm or did go back in time. Either way, I wanted to find the spear and hopefully a slingshot and be on my way.

The tree made me think it was a different realm. Like it was the transporter if you knew what you were doing. It only appeared dead to the untrained eye.

Not that I was trained but I had a habit of following hunches to my betterment.

Who was the owl though? That is the question.

Distracted by thoughts of the owl I didn't notice Ruad standing stock still leaning against one of the houses. He wrapped an arm around my waist as I walked past and pulled my back to his front as I squeaked in surprise. His familiar scent gave him away before I really went ballistic.

"What are you doing here?" I asked, annoyed, as I tried to writhe out of his grip.

"Hey, healer," he said as he tightened his grip.

"Do you need to assault me when you see me?"

"You wouldn't like me as much if I didn't."

He had me there.

"You forget I know everything," he said in my ear as he let me go.

"What are you doing here? In fact, why aren't you doing all of this since you can just pop in anytime, anywhere you want?" I said with vehemence.

I was madder that he called me out than that he was man-handling me. Smug bastard.

But I was glad he was here. I was more creeped out than I realized, his presence a sudden balm to my frayed nerves. Ignoring the itch to hold his hand or something stupid like that I crossed my arms over my chest and did my best glare.

"It has to be you. But I'm here to help."

"Lucky me," I grumbled. "And how are you going to do that? Is Declan okay?"

"Well, for starters I can keep you safe." He winked. "And secondly I can tell you that your friend Senan leaves clues. Third, yes he's fine."

Smug. But at least Declan was okay.

"Senan leaves clues, okay, and I have to find Senan to find the spear?"

"No grass growing in your pretty little head is there?"

I almost smacked him. But I thought better of it and looked around for clues.

I didn't see a yellow brick road or a rainbow so that was out. The ground was packed earth, well-worn with tuffets of grass here and there.

I didn't see any footprints, but it reminded me of a game path. My dad would teach me when I would go hunting with him, or when I did anything with him. I loved to learn, and he was a vat of knowledge.

But I remembered from those times that game paths were where animals would walk through the woods until there was an obvious path.

I guess this could be Senan's path, but the problem was, where did it lead? Left or right?

Following with my eyes I saw that to the left it led to one of the houses. The right led off around the bend where I couldn't see anymore.

It was less an obvious path but more a divot in the packed earth that was more prominent than the surrounding area. Walking over to the house that the path led to I tried glancing in a window.

Feeling like I was in a horror movie my adrenaline spiked uncomfortably in my veins. Ruad's hand was on my back before I had to reach out for him, and I breathed a little easier.

His much larger frame surrounded me as he peeked into the window with me.

No one jumped out at me at least, and I further relaxed into Ruad as I checked out the little house.

After another glance, we didn't see anyone inside for us to startle either. The modest inside was more of the packed dirt, with one table and one bed.

The bed had a threadbare quilt and the table only a single candle and an empty bowl with a spoon in it. Everything inside looked ancient. And lived in.

The hearth at the far end held ashes of a recent fire and you could smell the smoke clinging to the interior. There was still some liquid left in the bowl. The bed wasn't made but under the smoke smell was clearly a liquor smell and I think it emanated from the bed.

Tiptoeing I was trying to see more when Ruad lifted me up a little higher. That's when I saw the liquor bottles next to the bed. Definitely Senan then.

Tapping Ruad's arm to put me down I felt small. Not just in comparison to Ruad but in the grand scheme of things.

Centuries had passed since villages like this, and Senan I imagine was there for all of it. Ruad too.

Suddenly I felt the weight of those centuries, the lives gained and lost, the empires built and fallen.

"Aye, it's a heavy feeling, but it's enlightening too."

"How?"

"You appreciate the little things more. More than you can imagine."

"Doesn't seem like Senan does."

"Ah healer, no. Not everyone is blessed with a level head. But you know that already."

That I did.

"So where would he go from here?" I asked.

"Let's find out," he said as he swept his arm back the way we came with a flourish.

Leading the way I followed the trail as it wound its way through the little village. I kept feeling like something was going to happen but so far nothing.

"Are they afraid of you?" I asked.

His deep laughter left little doubt that they were.

"Knowledge is power," he said simply.

That it was.

"Then why aren't you with me all the time? That would make my life easier."

He wrapped a large hand around my smaller one.

"Are you questioning me?"

I rolled my eyes at him.

"While I would love to," he continued with a lascivious grin my way, "that's not how it works."

"Never is, is it?"

"You're stronger than you realize, Bridget."

I grunted a response. Yeah, sure I was.

As we continued our walk, I mused at how delightful this could be under different circumstances. While my heart was Declan's, Ruad was pleasant company all the same. Something few and far between in my experience.

I imagined us walking like this in a village exactly like this one, only in the period it belonged. Me wearing a work-worn dress. Ruad in a kilt. It was a nice thought. Like really nice.

"We've done this before haven't we?" I asked suddenly.

That feeling of needing him like I needed air was so strong, and so familiar. Like that pair of jeans you thought you lost, the denim hugged you like a long-lost friend. That's how that memory felt.

It could only be a memory. It was too real.

"Ah, but of course, my love. You always figure it out eventually."

"How many times? Do I always have to save the world?"

"You've done multiple different things over the centuries. Always saving this or that."

"Is that why you call me healer?"

"Yes and no. You know you're a triple deity, Brigid herself is. Over the years she can be more one thing than the other. She is what is needed.

"If the world needs to be bathed in fire, she is more the smith. When famine rocks the world she calls to the animals. The world today needs healing. But always you help. Whether it's with words, with wisdom, or by protecting those that need you. My healer."

"Yours?"

"Oh, you've belonged to me before. Maybe you will again. I am what you need me to be."

"Oh," I said for lack of anything else to say.

I felt a thrill in my stomach at his words that I tried to ignore. I was completely at a loss as to what to do with that information.

"It's alright, you know. I am what you need me to be. This journey you need Lugh because this time you need a savior yourself. I'm just happy to have a piece of you."

He brought our joined hands to his lips, bringing us to a halt as he did so. I felt like I had been flayed, not realizing the depth of my emotions until he had spoken the words out loud.

Left raw, his understanding was the death knell. I brought his hand to my lips, kissing his hand back as he had done mine. There was no adequate way of showing him how much he meant to me.

I knew my obsession with him was...different. Handsome was one thing, but I was unusually sensitive around him. It takes more than just a handsome face to keep my interest.

I guess now I know.

"Thank you for telling me all of that," I said softly, entranced by his gaze.

"Ah, no. Thank you beautiful. Declan is a lucky man. And one I will envy for years to come," he said with a wink.

I blushed, quite profusely, and ducked my head to break the spell he had me under. I was in so much trouble.

"All thoughts of loving you aside, we're here," he said as he pointed to the building we were stopped in front of.

The building was like the other but bigger, and the stench of stale alcohol was prevalent throughout. On the one side was a river that both provided the power, as it were, to the grinding of the grain as well as the water necessary to make some of it. An old mill and brewery then.

The trail we had been following was indeed leading to the door and went out of sight at the entrance. Seemed silly, like he was always walking to the liquor store, when he was a supernatural creature. But if he was protecting something inside, I guess it made sense.

"So what, we just walk in and grab it? Thanks have a nice day?" I asked Ruad. If it seems too good to be true, it usually is.

"Well Senan will be guarding it and to his nature, he will do every manner of trickery to shake you off its trail. It's up to you to figure fact from fiction."

"Can't you just go get it?"

"Just because I know everything does not mean I can do everything. No, this is for you and you alone."

"Any parting wisdom?"

"You don't have to be anything but what you are, healer," he said as he kissed my cheek.

Completely breathless after that, I realized I had a death grip on his hand. I really didn't want to let go. Of him, or of this moment, I wasn't totally sure.

But it wasn't only because I dreaded the task ahead of me.

I threw myself into his chest in a frenzy and wrapped my

arms around him like a boa constrictor. He didn't skip a beat as he wrapped his own around me tightly and kissed the top of my head. I gave him an answering one to his chest.

I really couldn't reach anywhere else, so I went with what was available.

"I will wait here for you," he said voice thick with emotion.

I nodded into his chest as I extracted myself. Looking up at him one last time I took a deep breath, gave him a nod, and went to face Senan.

# CHAPTER 11

Just because Ruad was what I needed him to be didn't mean it didn't take a toll on him. And just because I loved Declan didn't mean I didn't love Ruad. Just that it was different.

Or I was just fucked up.

Maybe both.

My head was in the clouds as I made my way into the building. Torn between lovers. More like torn between lives.

I used to be a different person. Not just the past lives I was somehow remembering. But in this actual life I used to be very different.

That person cared little for morals or who gave a fuck about her or what she did. She was little more than a wild animal. Trapped in a cage and fighting her way out.

Who I was now desperately cared for both of the men in my life. And I was breaking both of their hearts by doing so.

The smell of liquor hit me like a tsunami. My nostrils flared, and I took a huge gulp of the acrid air. It smelled sweet to me. The way cigarettes still smelled like Christmas morning after I quit.

Neither smell good to anyone but the addict.

My mouth watered and I could practically feel the liquor hit my stomach like a summer day. The way it slides down your throat and into your extremities like a warm caress.

I wanted it more than either man.

It called to me like a siren song and before I knew it I was staring down at rows of bottles. The amber liquid lit my blood on fire just looking at it.

I could feel my mouth salivate as my heartbeat tripled. Suddenly my mouth was a desert as the adrenaline coursed through my veins. Was I going to do this?

The severity of the situation doused me with cold water. Why was I debating this?

This whole situation had me on edge. Not just Ruad and Declan, or Carman, or Nick. The whole damn thing.

If I was being honest with myself I had felt the familiar itch since I saw Nick. That feeling like my skin was too tight, and I was going to burst with the effort to contain the crazy.

That's what Nick always did to me. It wasn't just his shittiness, though he was the worst. No, it was that feeling my family had always given me. Or a family member.

Knowing what was happening and being powerless to fight back.

That was the crazy that seeped out when I was at my worst. That was what Nick pulled out of me.

It was every fake smile, every backhanded compliment, all of the empty hugs that I was not allowed to speak out against.

I had to appreciate "everything" they did for me. Which was fucking squat.

What they did was stab me in the back when no one was looking and then cry wolf. Making me lose my temper so they could play the victim.

Brainwash my friends and family into thinking I was the loose cannon. Until I became the loose cannon they accused me of being.

But I took it. I took it all.

Believing I deserved their treatment. Thinking it was me that was worthless. That somehow I was asking them to abuse me.

I lied for them to protect my siblings from them. That's the truly insidious part of who they were. Forcing other people to take the blame for their shitty behavior.

Making my father make deals with me so I didn't out them.

It was always, "I know this was supposed to be your sweet sixteen but I promise I'll get you that Mustang you always wanted."

I'm twenty-four and still no Mustang.

Snapped back to reality I looked around for Senan. He was standing in the corner observing me quietly. For once he wasn't in his cups, but he was keen, staring me down.

It was a little unnerving. He shouldn't be capable of looks like that. It made me think of the owl.

"Clever," was all he said before poof he was gone.

I sincerely dreaded this.

Shaking off the vestiges of that sweet addiction calling my name, I checked out the room.

It was big, open, with barrels stacked up everywhere. The lighting came from huge windows filtering in natural light. The mill was over the river to the right of me, creating that wonderfully relaxing running water sound.

I zeroed in on that sound. Let the water cleanse my mind and spirit a moment while I continued to get my bearings.

Glancing back at the liquor bottles I could now see that they were dust-covered and grimy. Good enough reason not to drink some.

But it would be wonderful...

Water, okay water sound. Focus Bridget. Where did Senan go and where would the spear be stashed?

Wandering around aimlessly I made it to the other room that was dedicated mostly to storage and distribution. This was a fairly large-scale business here.

But if Senan was a customer, then it made sense. It had to distill for a long time too so maybe that was it.

The rafters were wooden logs, felled and split by craftsman long gone. All business, the building lacked any personal touches and was completely utilitarian. If it wasn't necessary, this building did not have it.

Which was the complete opposite of buildings of the Victorian era, I mused. With closets in closets and doors that led to secret rooms, none of that was here.

Which meant I had zip. Zip, zilch, nada. I didn't know what I was looking for or how to start looking for something to look for.

That had me thinking of what Ruad said about Senan tricking me. Was this a trick too?

I started knocking on walls and kicking floorboards looking for anything hollow sounding. When I got to the barrels, I knocked on them too. Some were full and some hollow.

The hollow ones were obvious. They were separate from the rest and clearly empty. But I kept knocking.

Halfway through the pile of full ones I knocked on one underneath another one that gave a resounding echo. Now that wasn't odd in itself if it weren't for the one on top being full. Quite like it was an attempt at hiding the hollow one.

Walking around it in a slow circle I saw a huge crack in one of the planks of wood. That could be why it was empty or that could be something.

Not wanting to rip my fingernails out prying this thing open I ran around until I found a crowbar. They had to use them here and sure enough, there was one in the corner.

Giving a good heave-ho, I expected it to pop right open. I don't know why I thought that.

Twenty minutes and multiple obscenities later I was in the middle of kicking the crowbar as it was wedged in the crack. Finally, it gave way after a really solid donkey kick. Like hands and knees, I gave it every bit of muscle I could muster without good leverage.

Taking the crowbar in hand and a few gulping breaths I went to peek inside. No liquid came pouring out, so I was glad that it was hollow.

Just from a distance, I could see only blackness. No Cheshire cat smiling back at me from the darkness, and no Senan either.

"If you drown yourself in the bottom of the barrel, there may be no coming out," Senan called from behind me.

"You're one to talk."

"Aye, you're right lass, you are. But there is no need to go in there. You have the spear."

What? Looking in my hand I saw the crowbar. I motioned toward it to Senan.

"This?" I asked incredulously.

"Aye. I'm not yanking your chain this time. Now come let's go. You got what you're after." He was motioning with his hands for me to join him.

"I have a crowbar, Senan. I don't see a spear,"

He was suddenly inches away from my face. His sobriety was less shocking than the fear I saw in his eyes. Both eyes were as big as saucers, the black swallowing the green that barely peeked through. Snapping his finger, he grabbed my hand with the crowbar.

"There, a spear, you see? Now let's get going, lass. Time's a wasting," he said as he pulled me to my feet.

Sure enough, there was a spear in my hand, one made for a man of Declan's height and weight. It felt awkward and obtrusive in my hand.

"Is this another trick though? Why just hand it to me?"

"There's much and more you don't understand. Now, let's go."

"Was it the barrel? What was going to happen when I went in there?"

"No, lass, that's just child's play. Makes you feel like you lost your marbles, but you haven't. No, she wants you and I don't want to be in her crosshairs. Best get you back to Ruad, now come."

"She? Carman?"

"I've said enough," he said with finality as he pulled me again.

Ruad was there before we made it to the door. Senan all but threw me at him and backed away like I was on fire.

"Go! Take her. I'll be the fool that I am. Hurry!" Senan shout-whispered at Ruad.

"Thank you," was Ruad's fervent response as he ushered me out.

"What's going on?" I asked.

"Not now, keep moving I'll explain it all when we're back," Ruad said without a glance my way.

Our quiet peaceful walk on the way in was a mad dash on the way out. We blew past the buildings before Ruad gave up and picked me up and took off at what felt like warp speed to me.

In the blink of an eye we were back on our side of the fence. I was clutching Ruad white-knuckled, spear behind his back and my head buried in his neck. I could see the owl, impassive as ever, through the crook of his neck, perched on his dead tree.

Maybe it wasn't Senan.

Ruad relaxing was my cue that I could too, and I slowly loosened my grip. He passed me to Declan's waiting arms, and I looked up expectantly, ducking my head a little expecting his ire.

Concern etched his features and in his eyes was confusion and a little fear. My heart melted like ice cream at the beach, and I gave him a big kiss before composing myself.

"What happened?" Declan boomed, moving from my face to Ruad's.

"There's more to the story than originally disclosed," he said a little sheepishly.

Was he unsure of himself? That was highly uncharacteristic. I whipped my head around to look at him.

He stared at me through thick lashes, looking apologetic. And more than a little uncomfortable.

"Ruad, if you know everything, are you just toying with us then?" I said.

"Ugh, no. It's more like I know the possibilities, but I have to wait for them to happen. I can't tell you what you will say next but sometimes based on what you say I know what should happen later. Does that make sense?"

"Following," I said, still in Declan's arms.

"And these things are cycles. Some big and some small. Tons of different ones. They leave patterns that I can recognize but I'm not omnipotent, only knowledgeable of the patterns."

"So what cycle is this one?"

"Not the one I was looking forward to. A big one. And Carman is just the beginning."

"Who was Senan talking about?"

"The Faerie Queen."

"Oh bollocks, the Faerie Queen, what are you getting at now?"

Declan exploded.

His outburst took both Ruad and me by surprise and we both stared at him. He was shaking a little more visibly and his Irish complexion was red with pent-up emotion.

"Let's go back and I can explain more," Ruad said.

He seemed uneasy, and I glanced at Declan. He seemed to be settling. Reassured that the tension was dissipating I tapped Declan to put me down.

Ruad came up to us before he could and placed a hand on each of us. Suddenly we were back at the edge of the woods, golf cart and all.

"Can you do that more? It would save me a lot of time," I said to Ruad.

He only looked at me in answer, but he said, "Hurry back to the house. I'll be waiting," and he was gone.

Looking at Declan I felt the weight of my walk with Ruad hanging between us. But there wasn't time for that right now.

He placed me in the cart gently and stared at me a moment. Grabbing my face with both hands he kissed me gently on the lips, then on my cheek, and finally on my forehead.

"You have to stop disappearing on me," he said, voice thick and gravelly.

"I'm sorry, I didn't mean to," I said as I brought him down for another kiss.

"I know, love, I know," he said as he made his way to the driver's side of the cart.

The quiet stretched between us as he drove back to the main office. It didn't feel hostile or upset, maybe just tired. I let it be, grateful for a moment to recharge after so much activity.

He returned what we needed to while I beelined for the car. I could hardly walk in there with a spear taller than Declan and even at that I had to try to hide it in with the golf clubs as we drove to avoid people noticing it. I had crept around the back of the building while he went inside and I all but sprinted to the car when no one could be seen in the lot.

Once in the car, I had to jimmy it awkwardly in between the

car seats, with the bottom at my feet on the passenger side and the tip in the ceiling of the backseat. I hoped it didn't tear the roof apart.

Sitting in the car by myself I felt guilty. Guilty for loving two men, guilty for almost succumbing to the pull of escape, ashamed of who I was.

Unadulterated rage for people that made me feel that way.

While I ruminated it only made me want to do something destructive even more. My skin felt like it was crawling with thousands of ants, too tight to hold in all of this anxiety welling up inside of me.

When Declan got in the car, there was a pregnant pause. Both of us knew something needed to be said but what?

"How long was I gone for?" I asked after a moment.

"Maybe a half an hour," he said staring through the windshield, not moving.

"About Ruad..." I began when he held up a hand.

Holding my breath, his went out in a whoosh. I could tell he was gathering his thoughts, so I waited.

"I have to tell you something," he began, "but best I show you first."

He took out his phone and fiddled with it a second or two before handing it to me.

"Go on, read," he said.

And so I did. It was more about Brigid, a screenshot of a website detailing her life and characteristics. As I neared the bottom I saw what I assumed he meant. Listed as Brigid's son was a boy by the name of Ruadán.

My stomach did funny things as my mind came up with implications.

"Declan..." I said pained. There I go again ruining things.

"Oh, Bridget, no," he said as he kissed my hand. "I should have told you sooner, only I didn't know exactly."

"Why would you need to tell me?"

"Darling, a man looks differently at the woman he loves. I knew it the moment he saw you he was a goner. Only, now I know you know it too."

"Declan, I'm sorry."

"For what, love? You've done nothing wrong. You can't help your feelings in this mess,"

"But it hurts you."

"Oh, it's not so much that it hurts me. It's that I know it hurts you."

"Me?"

"Bridget, it pains me to know you feel like you're letting the both of us down, but I assure you, you're not. Ruad and I have already had our own talk on the matter, and I know he's taken a step back for us. I need you to know I'm alright with it, well, the way that it is. I'd be lying if I said I would take a step back," he said with a wink.

"Declan," I started. I couldn't finish before tears started in my eyes.

"Oh hush now, no need for all of that. It's almost a relief to know you've got someone to protect you when I can't. Someone to comfort you and help you. I trust you, Bridget, more than I thought possible, but those reasons for having difficulty trusting aren't related to you. You've proven to me you were worthy of trusting time and again. And damn it if I don't trust you with everything that I've got despite myself."

"Declan." This time words weren't entirely necessary, and I was grateful for it because I couldn't speak beyond the lump in my throat.

I threw myself at him, wrapping my arms tightly around his neck. Kissing him fervently I pulled back after a few moments.

"I don't deserve you," I whispered.

"You're stuck with me all the same," he whispered back.

"Good. I'm glad," I said with a chuckle.

"Me too," he said kissing me again before turning the car on and heading out.

The car ride went uneventfully and maybe too quickly. After the initial relief at Declan's complete acceptance, I started feeling guilty for not telling him about the liquor. How I almost succumbed to temptation.

Now it felt like a burden on a good mood, and I didn't think it was the time to share it. Besides, he knew what it was like, and I didn't think putting the bug in his ear about it was the kindest thing to do. Still, it stuck in my craw a little.

I let my mind drift with the landscape flying by until I was numb with it. Numb felt like the way to go. Before I knew it we were back at the house, and I had to shake some of the fog off so I could be present for this next talk.

Ruad was waiting for us when we came inside, Failinis at his side like old pals. He gave us a small smile, and I felt more guilt again.

What had become of the son we shared in another life? I would have to ask him another time.

There was no missing the unspoken exchange between them this time. Or the slight fall in Ruad's countenance.

He recovered quickly though and turned his smile up to one hundred for my benefit. I smiled back, appreciating the sentiment. He only wanted to make me feel better.

"Now then," Ruad began, "I believe this calls for some tea."

Taking my cue I left the men to it as I started the kettle. I could hear Ruad filling Declan in on our time in Senan's world, glossing over the battle with the liquor I'm certain he knew happened. Grateful for his discretion, I marveled at their ability to work together despite the obvious.

Counting my lucky stars, I took the tea and some food out to them. Two handsome, smiling faces met my entrance, and I had a hard time believing I was worth it. But I would take it.

"Alright, hit me," I said as I put the tray down.

"Faerie Queen, yes. Well, it's like I said. There are cycles, but I usually don't know them straightaway. I'm here when the world needs me and if not I'm in our world. Like Asgard for the Norse Gods, or Mount Olympus for the Greeks.

"There are folks that have my traits like the both of you have Brigid and Lugh's. But the Gods themselves usually remain in our world unless need be. We let you handle lots of things on your own.

"I thought it strange to be here. It's been quite some time since I have. Even stranger that Brigid and Lugh are here in full force. It's like I said, usually your kind would get a little of this and a little of that. The Faerie Queen being here makes sense of all that.

"She is exactly what you would expect, the queen to the faeries. Capricious, egocentric, and mad as a hatter. I should have been tipped off by the power of the two of you."

"I mean that's not what I would've expected," I said.

"What would you think the Faerie Queen would be?"

"Maybe benevolent, kind, revered?"

"True enough in days long gone but centuries ago she took a hard left turn and never came back. Beautiful, she is, deadly as well.

"She comes around to cause mayhem and destruction every now and again and is the reason Carman and company are back.

"To this point I hadn't known she was around. There has been chaos in the other realm that no one had been able to pinpoint. But no one else besides the queen has the power to spring people from the depths of hell, never mind the audacity.

"The problem with her causing chaos isn't just the chaos itself. When she has one of these *fits,* she always takes a mortal lover.

"While that's not a problem in and of itself, it's that she always pays a tithe to hell by sacrificing her mortal lovers. That's how she gets the strings to pull people out of hell. And now I know whom she wants to take."

Surely not me...

"Declan?" I asked.

"That is my suspicion, yes," Ruad answered.

"Okay but then why did you rush me out of Senan's world like you did?" I asked.

"Well, mad she may be, but not stupid. She knows Declan won't go willingly, and that's why she wants him. Lugh was a High King in his day, and the Queen of Elphame wants power more than anything. But she knows his loyalty. The key to controlling him is you, my love."

I glanced at Declan, and he laughed.

"I just genuinely can't see how you're both just fine with this," I said.

"That's what you're worried about right now?" Declan said.

"It defies nature."

"Darling, I think it's that you've been with boys your whole life. Now you're with men," Ruad said with finality.

Well, alright then. Declan laughed again.

"What?" I asked.

"He said it best, darling," he said with a wink.

I didn't miss that they had both used the same endearment. It was a little weird, but it worked I guess.

"So, that is why I hightailed you out of there. Declan can more or less hold his own. The spear will help him tremendously and both Failinis and Enbarr would help if he needed it. You are more vulnerable, especially if you don't know what to do, but that's why you have me.

"In Senan's world, you were particularly vulnerable because that is her domain. Senan alerted me as soon as he felt her presence and I came to get you out of there and he stalled," Ruad finished.

"Well, but hold on, is Senan good or bad?"

"Senan is a complicated fellow. Clurichauns are like leprechauns only drunk and miserable. They protect treasure like your spear, but if you had to guard something for centuries, you would be bored too.

"So he drinks and plays tricks on folks for fun. But they can be helpful when they want to. They don't mean harm, but they won't necessarily stop you from harming yourself."

He glanced at me at that, and I did my best to remain stoic. His words were only in acknowledgment of the situation, exempt from judgment.

Just a nod to say he knew and if I wanted to talk, he was there. I really was too lucky.

"Senan is an old friend. I think you all will get along famously. But do watch over him for me?"

"What? He's joining the entourage?" I asked.

"Well, you have the spear. And he may owe me a few favors. He will help me watch over you both."

"Dependable babysitter?" Declan inquired.

It was a valid concern.

"One of the best," Ruad answered.

Declan grunted. Yeah, I wasn't sold on that either.

"So why are we watching over him? And now, correct me if I'm wrong, but this Queen of Elphame is the reason Carman is after me?" I said.

"More or less. If Carman succeeds in getting you out of the picture, Declan is the queen's for the taking. And if she doesn't the queen is in the same predicament. Except if Carman doesn't succeed she'll have to roll up her sleeves to do the job. And she really hates that.

"And poor old Senan is just a little misunderstood. You can appreciate that."

Couldn't I ever.

"What do we do?" I asked.

"Tonight you relax. I don't anticipate any activity yet. This was only her first grab, and it was a convenient one.

"Carman will be mourning her son's passing. I imagine it will take a little more than a night to recover. Unless she comes in a fit of rage, but we're prepared all the same.

"The queen's presence is a concern. It means she thinks Carman will fail, which is good, but her already going after you means she's impatient. And desperation leads to irrationality. Which makes her difficult to predict.

"I think what the queen didn't plan on was me, and that's a good thing. It's a good thing because I don't think she has figured out that I'm here yet. Which gives us the element of surprise.

"All in all we're in good shape. She may suspect Senan, but if you're watching his back, and me yours, we'll be fine. If you need me call. The tea was perfect," he said as he stood up, kissed my head, and was gone.

"How do I call you?" I said to the empty air.

"Still hung up on that?" Declan said.

I just shrugged. But seriously how did I call him?

I felt bad when he kissed me in front of Declan, even if it was only on my head. But I felt worse because I wanted him to.

After all of the intimacy we had shared today I would have felt bereft if he hadn't. This was so messed up.

"Relax, will you? Does he kiss you like this?" Declan said as he turned my body toward his and kissed me like a man starved.

"Hmm, I'm not sure. Maybe if you do it again I'll be certain," I said stupidly, breathlessly, when he pulled away.

His answering growl was the desired effect. As he scooped me into his arms, I thought that maybe things would be alright.

* * *

I woke to a stream of curse words to make a sailor blush. It was pitch black and as disoriented as I was I knew that wasn't Declan's voice. Sure enough, he was sound asleep next to me.

The smell of whiskey told me who the voice was, and I sat up to see Senan trying to right a dresser he had knocked into. He was picking up the objects that had fallen and were scattered all over the place.

"Senan, what is it?" I whispered as loudly as I could.

He continued to mutter curse words while cleaning up the mess he had made. When he finally looked up at me he rushed over.

"Lass, up with you now," he slurred at full volume.

"Shhh! Why? What's going on?" I asked. Declan was still fast asleep and Senan was over here making a racket.

"He won't be waking up anytime soon, lass."

"What? What are you talking about?"

I grabbed Declan's shoulder and gave it a shake. Nothing. The sound of his deep breathing kept me from completely panicking, but I tried to wake him again.

The only indication that he noticed was a change in his breathing. It picked up the pace for a few moments before resuming the deep even breaths of sleep.

"Hexed," Senan said simply.

"Hexed? But what about the warding at the door? And the knot he had drawn on him?"

I grabbed his arm to look for the knot and sure enough, it was faded right through the center. We have to get these damn things tattooed on us next.

"Magic like that is dormant until activated. Carman must have done the spell after she figured we were all settled so it wasn't evil until then. The knot I suppose was taken care of while you were under Darkness's spell. It was the only time myself or Ruad were not watching Declan,"

His brogue was worse for the slurring, but he was sobering up by the second. I was having a hard time shaking the sleep that had been disturbed. Senan placed a hand on my shoulder and the magic that erupted between us woke me up instantly.

"What was that?" I asked, pulling back. It was like an electric shock.

"Just a touch of magic. You need to wake up and so do I," he said, words crystal clear this time.

"What does it sober you up?" I asked, fully alert now.

"Aye, that one does. We need to be on the lookout now. They're going to be trying something and I won't lose either of you."

I was a little taken aback by his words. His fervor for our safety was touching.

"Oh, you didn't think this old coot had a heart, did ya?" he said with a wink.

"I mean, no that's not it. I just didn't know we mattered all that much."

"A lad and a lass like you are all that matters in this world. Now come, we have to prepare. Ruad will be here soon."

He handed me the salt that Joan had given me.

"Place a circle around Declan, be quick about it," he said as he pulled the bed out from the wall.

God but he was strong for a little thing.

I did as he said, going as fast as I could while making the salt a thick line around the bed. Lucky it was as big a container as you could get because it made it, even though I worried about it halfway through. Senan was busy doing what I could only assume was magic in the corner, hands in a flurry of motion in the direction of Declan and me.

"Now what?" I asked.

"Now we look for the hex bag," Ruad's voice said from behind me.

My stomach did a flip-flop as I looked at him. His face was impassive, the normal ease of expression, a cold mask.

I averted my eyes quickly, not wanting to put my emotions on him. It was time for business not emotions.

Tiptoeing over the salt line I started checking Declan's person and the bed while the two of them tore apart the room. I was on my second round over Declan when commotion could be heard from the window. Failinis was howling while Enbarr could be heard whinnying.

"Times up folks," Senan mumbled.

# CHAPTER 12

I looked up at Ruad and instantly regretted it. He looked murderous, and it didn't do wonders for my sense of panic that was slowly rising.

"Ruad?" I croaked, voice hoarse with sleep and fear.

He crossed the room in three huge strides, careful not to break the salt line as he did so. Taking my face in his hands he kissed my forehead. The rage still simmered, but he gave me a reassuring look as he continued to hold my head in his hands.

"We can't eliminate Carman, not without Declan, but we can knock her back a few pegs. Stay inside with Senan. You're of more use to him if you stay close."

He was already walking away when I pulled him back by his shirt. When he turned to face me, I threw my arms around him and buried my face in his neck. He wrapped his own completely around my waist as he kissed my hair.

Okay, just a little emotion.

"It'll be alright," he whispered.

"Just stay safe, please," I whispered around the lump in my throat.

As I pulled back, I kissed his cheek. Despite myself, a tear escaped and Ruad wiped it away with the pad of his thumb. He gave me a small smile, nodded at Senan, who nodded militantly back, and he was gone.

I wasn't sure why I was so rattled. The safety and comfort both men offered me was something I hadn't realized I was already so used to.

And sending Ruad to protect Declan felt like sacrificing one for the other. Both of these things left me feeling very off-kilter.

Senan's face was suddenly right in front of mine, snapping me out of my self-pity. His worried expression cleared as his face swam into focus.

"There ye are, lass. No time for that now, we need to find that hex bag. Ruad can do damage, to be sure, but this is black magic we're dealing with not just some faerie dust."

Nodding numbly I went back to task. While Senan rifled through drawers and looked over and under different pieces of furniture, I kept looking through the bed and Declan's clothes.

"Wait, why would there be a hex bag over there? I thought no one could get inside?" I asked, the thought suddenly hitting me.

"No one *could*," a voice said from the hallway, accentuating the past tense.

From the darkness of the hallway, a face began to appear. Evil. A moment later, a second face was illuminated by the light from the window.

It was Nick.

The latter at least had the gumption to look ashamed of himself. Evil looked like the cat that got in the cream.

"You fucking idiot," I spat at Nick.

His recoil almost made me feel bad for him. Almost, not quite.

"Ah, he's not the sharpest tool in the shed, I'll grant you, but he's sharp enough," Evil said, smirking at Nick at his side.

Evil touched Nick on the shoulder and whispered something inaudible. What cognizance was on Nick's face was wiped instantly and he looked more like a robot than a person. Headed straight for me, I could only assume what Evil's directive had been.

Senan started conjuring up some magic but was halted by Evil. With the brutality denoting his name, he threw Senan into a dresser with the flick of his wrist, allowing Nick to pass him on his journey toward me.

I'd like to say this was the first time Nick looked at me like that, advancing on me with only ill intentions.

The panic that shot through me was similar too. I crawled backward on the bed, arms raised to protect myself.

I couldn't believe this was happening again. How badly I wished Declan were awake right now. Declan needed to wake up.

With the thought of Declan, I came to myself a little. It wasn't long after Nick that Declan came into my life. And I'm not the girl I was when I was with Nick, not anymore.

The rage that erupted from me was unlike anything I had ever felt before.

Fuck Nick.

He can't touch me without my permission.

Nope, I was Declan's now.

Declan wouldn't be with a pushover.

Looking around for a weapon I could use I noticed that Senan did not seem to be winning his battle. I only hoped that he could hang on long enough for me to get through Nick.

Not finding a worthy weapon, it was too late. As Nick crawled onto the bed after me I did the only thing I could think of. Saying a quick prayer for help to my bracelet I hoped for the best as he tried to wrap his hands around my throat.

The panic came but this time I was able to abate it. I had a life worth fighting for, damn it, and I fought hard to get it. This asshole wasn't going to take it from me. No one was.

Never again.

I kicked him with a force he wasn't prepared for, knocking him onto the floor, if only for a moment. A moment was all I needed.

Taking the offensive, I went after him like a woman possessed, the irony not escaping me. One solid thwack to his temple put him back on the floor and I straddled him to get the leverage I needed.

Wrapping my hands around his throat I prayed for the strength to knock him out, hoping it would be good enough to break the spell. He might be an asshole, but he didn't deserve to die, especially not like this.

As he fought, writhing underneath me, I wasn't sure I would

have the strength to hold him much longer.

Suddenly I saw the panic in his eyes, and I eased up, just enough to allow a gulp of air.

I shouldn't have.

He took the moment of reprieve to yank my hair backward like the worm that he was. I wasn't letting go that easy though.

My fingers were losing purchase, so I dug the balls of my feet into the ground. The worst thing I could do was give him the upper hand.

As I fought for purchase, I was barely aware of Senan until he crashed into the two of us. Lying there, sprawled out on my back I fought for air while Senan scrambled to get off of me.

Blinking away black spots, I was leaning up when I saw Evil going to get Declan. Jumping to my feet I paused when Evil did. Nick and Senan were a tangled mess, both struggling to get their bearings.

My brain was pretty slow still, so I looked around to see why he had stopped when I saw the salt. After all of this nonsense it was miraculously unbroken, Declan still in a heavy slumber on the bed.

I vaulted over the salt line, really much harder than was necessary but I was trying to be quick. Evil flashed a look of abhorrence my way as I reached Declan's sleeping figure.

The time for sanity was long gone, and I tore clothes off of him with alacrity. Every second was painful as I still didn't find the hex bag and my movements grew frantic.

"Little girl, what makes you think you can win this anyway?" Evil said from behind the salt line.

I didn't honor him with a response.

There was only his underwear left, and I was hoping to save him his integrity, so I ran my hands all over them first. Finally, I felt a lump on the material on his inner thigh.

Going for broke I put my teeth to the material and tore at it like a fishing line. Honestly, it didn't stand a chance, and it tore away from his boxer briefs so easily I fell backward. Nothing happened.

"Senan!" I shouted. He would know what to do.

Holding the hex bag in the air, sewn into the hem of his damn underwear I felt like a lunatic. You know those moments in life that you ask yourself, wait how did I get here? This was one of them.

Senan said a few words in Gaelic and the bag exploded into flames in my hand. I threw it at Nick.

Just at his feet. I wasn't looking to hurt him. Maybe scare him a little.

Evil gave an unearthly roar that startled us all, Declan the most. He sprang up from the bed, all flustered and flailing limbs.

Locking eyes with him I tried to calm him down and warn him at the same time. He was safe, for now. I think he got it.

"You rotten bitch!" Evil snarled at me.

Suddenly Senan was thrown back into the wall, eyes bulging. I was ready to throw myself at Evil when Declan cautioned me with a hand on my shoulder.

My temper had reached the boiling point though. Senan was struggling, and he needed me. This ended now.

Closing my eyes I said another silent prayer. Focusing all of my energy on helping get my loved ones out of this I felt a little twinge and I latched onto it.

Opening my eyes, there were thousands of tiny firefly-like lights flying around the room.

Like the ones that helped Brian and grew on the ivy, they swarmed Evil, covering every inch of him.

He started swatting at the areas they were accumulating but it did no good. As they grew in number, he grew in frustration and was throwing himself into the wall in a flurry.

"What are you doing to me?" he screeched.

I had no idea what I was doing, so I didn't answer. Instead, I continued to focus on the feeling I felt, that twinge that told me not to give up yet.

Something was happening to Evil though. He looked like he was sinking into himself.

Senan was on the floor recovering, as was Nick now. Senan

waved a hand after another few seconds and ivy sprung through the floorboards, winding its way up Evil's body. Like his brother, the ivy wrapped around him until the magic snuffed out what was left of his life as I and Senan controlled it.

When it was over, and the fireflies returned to me it took a while longer for my skin to stop glowing like the first time. I was still on high alert and when Declan touched my arm, I nearly jumped out of my skin.

"Bridget, relax. He's gone. What happened?" Declan said softly, treating me like a wild animal.

I felt like a wild animal.

Declan was pulling me softly toward him, but I wasn't budging, still fixated on Evil's now lifeless form. He was already back to dirt and plants.

It was Nick's voice that broke my trance.

"I'm sorry," he whispered.

I lost my shit.

I vaulted toward him, but Declan caught me by the waist before I could reach him.

"You're sorry!? You're right you're fucking sorry!" I spat at him.

Years of pent-up anger at him came spewing from me. Like spitting out venom that had poisoned me back at the snake. I couldn't tell you what I said, all I saw was red as I gave Nick every ounce of rage I hadn't realized I still held onto.

Nick never raised his head. He kept his eyes on the floor as he took every insult I could think of. When the storm was finally over I slumped into Declan like a deflated balloon.

"Bridget, I know I deserved that and then some. I hope you know I truly am sorry," Nick said, looking at me for the first time.

I might have felt guilty if he hadn't apologized like that too many times before. That's how people like him operate.

They're so sorry and they'll never do it again.

Until they do.

Then it's the last time, they swear.

Sure.

Then it was my fault they did it again.

Never their fault.

Why didn't I know that they were going to be at home that night? After they told me they were going out.

Surely I'm to blame for not knowing they changed their plans when they didn't tell me.

Why didn't I rearrange my life to accommodate them?

Of course, I deserve to be punished for not being able to read their minds. And for not changing my plans when I didn't know I had to!

How dare I.

Blame the whole damn universe before they admit they did anything wrong.

As if the cosmos lined up just right for them to completely destroy me again.

At this point I knew it wasn't *just* Nick I was mad at, but it was him who was in front of me at the moment.

He was saved by the ruckus outside the window.

In a sense, so was I. Spiraling was never fun. And I was moments away from free-falling.

"Ruad," I said, looking at Declan.

Finally remembering what I had to hold on to. Who, more like.

"Explain on the way," he said, jumping up and pulling me with him.

God, I was lucky.

It's all about perspective, isn't it?

I saw Senan push Nick toward the door and sent him a glance of thanks. Mad, sure, but I knew I couldn't let Nick out of my sight.

I explained as quickly and breathlessly as possible as we flew through the house. We were rounding the front door when Declan grabbed the spear.

In hindsight maybe we should have brought it to the bedroom with us, but we were thinking this was going to be an easy night. So much for that.

On the front porch, Enbarr was on us in a flash. Declan threw me up before he vaulted onto him. I almost felt bad for the horse, but he was a behemoth and didn't so much as flinch when Declan landed.

Without a saddle or reins, I was left with only his mane to clutch and to squeeze my thighs as my life depended on it, literally. Declan was behind me, holding onto my waist.

I couldn't see Ruad, but I could hear Failinis barking like crazy. Enbarr wasted no time. Trusting us to remain seated he was off like the wind.

The air was charged with electricity. The way it feels right before a thunderstorm in the summer, that heavy feeling like the air is somehow too thick. As we neared the battlefield, I could see why.

The magic in the air was palpable, giving off the thunderstorm feeling and making the back of my throat itch with its density. A black cloud was visible above the two opponents as Ruad and Carman exchanged blows.

It was a flurry of activity, each of them waving their hands around and flinching in turn. There were no wands. These two were magic embodied as they hurled attacks at each other.

From the motions, it seemed like Ruad was losing. He was visibly battered, bruises on his arms and scratches here and there. Every attack he mounted she countered with feline precision. A simple wave of a hand, a duck, a step to the side. She had a few marks herself but was otherwise not phased.

Ruad by contrast was breathing heavily, being knocked to his knees a time or two that I could see. It was when he was knocked clear on his ass that I nearly jumped off Enbarr and took off running.

Declan felt the tension in my body and before I could make the jump, he cautioned me with a squeeze.

"I need you to keep Enbarr steady. Head straight for Carman, and don't rear up until I say so," he yelled in my ear.

I nodded my acknowledgment, not trusting he could hear my voice over the wind whipping past us. Not at all certain I could control Enbarr if my life depended on it, but I would try.

I knew enough to steer him and by some stretch of luck, the horse understood what I meant. Declan was clutching my shoulders, having removed his hands from my waist, and I could feel him adjusting. Figuring out what he meant to do, I hunched my head down a little.

He would have one shot at this.

Holding my shoulder with his left hand and placing his left knee against my behind, he raised his right leg for leverage and raised the spear with his right hand. It was an impossible situation and one I didn't imagine he could maintain for long, so I squeezed Enbarr tighter and said a little prayer.

We needed all the luck we could get.

I could feel Declan pull back as he was ready to let the spear loose, and I bit my lip in a ridiculous attempt to help steer it. Like how when I bowl, and I lean my body sideways as if it will tilt the world on its axis to help me get a spare.

Holding my breath and staying as stock still as you can on a galloping horse I felt Declan as he threw the spear full throttle at Carman. Both fighters were too focused to even notice our presence. While I watched the spear sail through the air, I bit my tongue praying it hit its mark.

Ruad noticed it flying through the air. It was a barely there turn of his head, but it was enough. Carman whipped her head in the direction of the spear as Ruad sent a particularly nasty spell her way to keep her busy. She reacted like she had been struck by lightning, head thrown back, arms outstretched, as she gave an unearthly howl.

The spear hit her in the leg.

The leg.

I waited with bated breath praying to all things holy that it was enough. As the spell ended she gave a murderous look toward Declan, now seated again. With a grimace she grabbed the spear with two hands and gave it a tug.

It stayed put.

In her moment of inattention and frustration, I saw a figure launch out of the woods behind her. Failinis launched at her like a hell hound and latched onto her neck. With a brutal shake of his head, Carman's body went limp.

Declan had patted my waist, my sign to halt Enbarr. I steered him toward Carman's body at a walk, watching for signs of life.

Failinis stalked his prey still, sniffing here and there, finding her unsavory. His muzzle was slick with blood, and for the first time, I felt genuine fear looking at him. In truth, he was massive, and when he circled her, there was something feral about him.

When he looked up at me, I jumped ever so slightly. Failinis didn't mind. He glanced down impassively, continuing his survey. I kind of minded; I hated fearing anything.

Ruad wasn't moving. My peripheral vision was hyper-aware of that fact. Now that the immediate threat seemed to be taken care of, I attempted to swing down to attend Ruad when Declan stopped me.

"Stay here," was all he said.

Not particularly in the mood to argue, I let him go. He was capable and would take care of Ruad. And, well, maybe Failinis still looked like he was on the hunt, and I liked sitting astride Enbarr for now.

So sue me.

I was reticent to break my concentration of Carman and Failinis, but I could see the tension in Declan as he hunched over Ruad. Turning their way, I locked eyes with Declan. His expression was confused and worried, so I turned Enbarr their way and got closer.

"What is it?" I asked. My voice sounded small to my ears, far away.

"I don't know. I can't see any injuries that would keep him unconscious, but he's breathing," Declan said.

"Darkness has a hold of him," Senan said from behind us.

"So go get him like you did for me," I said a little impatiently.

"I'm trying but something's blocking me. Some warding I don't recognize."

"What do you mean? What do we do?" I asked.

They both looked at me, then each other. No one had anything to offer.

"Well, doesn't he have a physical body somewhere?" I asked.

I imagined his magic being like a skinwalker, his physical body residing somewhere while his ethereal body inhabited another's. Less like *Supernatural* and the body snatchers and more like *Game of Thrones* and the Wildlings. Where the body snatchers shed their skin to take on a new form, the Wildlings could embody animals they were connected to, spirits sharing the animal's body.

"Right you are," mumbled Senan.

"So the three of you take Enbarr and find his body. Let Failinis lead the way and I can stay with Ruad," I said.

"No, you need to have someone here with you. Failinis stay here," Declan barked.

"But you need to find him fast! Failinis is your best bet!" I protested.

"Lass, I have to agree with the lad here. It would do us no good worrying about you. Keep Failinis with you and I will know if you need us," Senan said.

"Fine," I conceded. "But go quickly!"

With that, they were gone. Declan astride Enbarr in his briefs was a most absurd sight, and when he swung Senan up behind him, I almost laughed.

Almost.

Watching Nick run behind them was satisfying at least. He had no shot of keeping up but I was just glad he wasn't near me.

Looking down at Ruad the ache in my chest reached a fever pitch. It was easy to squelch it because we weren't out of danger, but it was there. Time for that later.

I didn't know what would happen if Darkness didn't relinquish him. But I was pretty sure I wouldn't like it.

Doing a thorough once over, I couldn't see any wounds on Ruad that concerned me. Scrapes and bruises littered his muscular torso, but none were severe.

Running my hands over his chest, I couldn't feel anything

broken beneath. I let my hands linger, enjoying the feel of the coarse dark hair that covered his chest and accentuated his physique.

It wasn't really the time for it but what the hell else was I supposed to do right now?

"Please wake up," I whispered.

Failinis was a statue beside me, only his ear twitching belied his alertness. His blood-soaked jowls were more gruesome up close, and I could smell the coppery scent of blood in the air. I was glad he was here.

Ruad's face twisted into a grimace, and I jumped to soothe him. Running my hands through his hair, it was velvety and thick. I marveled at its color as I whispered sweet nothings to him. I always thought it was duller but this close the deep bronze color shimmered.

God but he was handsome. Thick lashes and full lips, broad cheeks, and a square jaw. Even without the mirth that always existed on his features he was a sight to behold.

And he was big. As tall as Declan but all lean, hard muscles to Declan's stockiness. More like a swimmer to Declan's boxer physique.

Declan was a knockout artist if I ever saw one. Ruad was more a viper, quick and deadly.

I felt stupid. And useless. I'm over here ogling Ruad instead of taking any action. But I knew I was doing an important job, nonetheless.

Situating his head on my lap I held him more closely as I closed my eyes. Praying to all the faeries, magical creatures, and God alike I asked them to help Ruad out of this.

I stroked my hands over his hair and his face as I rocked him and prayed. Warmth flooded me as memories of him came to mind. His playfulness, his honesty, his realness. He was one of the rare ones who was exactly who they said they were.

Like Declan.

Memories came to me from other times too. I wasn't sure if it was my imagination or if I was remembering past lives or what.

Hell, maybe I was seeing Ruad's memories for all I knew.

Flashes of us holding hands in a meadow, us warming up near a fire, a toddler's face. That last one set off alarms in my head. The face looking a lot like Ruad.

As the love for both men overwhelmed me, I couldn't stop a few tears from escaping. I couldn't bear to lose either of them, and I felt perilously close to just that.

There was so much more I wanted to know from Ruad. I had so many questions that only he could answer. And selfishly, I just wanted to keep him around.

Opening my eyes, I had to blink away tears to be sure I wasn't mistaken. Millions of those tiny fireflies were flowing out of me and covering Ruad like glitter. More than I had ever seen before, they covered him in a fine dust of shimmering gold. My skin was the color of bronze, like his hair.

Asking for a little luck I leaned in to kiss him. It worked for *Disney* princesses, so why not me? Even though it was reversed. Gender roles be damned.

When our lips touched I wasn't sure what to expect. He was unconscious, after all. It was like kissing a wall. Just cold and uncompromising.

Well so much for that idea.

"Why did you stop?" Ruad said from my arms.

I was so relieved a sob escaped from somewhere in my chest.

"Hey, my love, it's alright. You didn't truly think I would leave you so soon, did you?" Ruad said softly as he lifted my chin with a finger.

This time he kissed me. Just a peck, but it was warm and firm and familiar. My breath hitched, with what I wasn't sure. I was ready to cry again when Ruad sat up and gathered me in his arms and held me close.

"No, love, it's over. Just breath. It's alright," he crooned as he smoothed my hair back from my face.

All of the adrenaline of the past few hours came crashing down at once. As I curled further into Ruad's embrace, I tried to focus on his scent. Very woodsy and spicy, I could smell the magic on him when I focused like this. It was sharp like vinegar but pleasant, more like concentrated cinnamon.

I was still aglow with fireflies, and they danced around Ruad and myself, keeping us in a little cocoon of light. A surge of love for Ruad pulsed through me and the fireflies danced around quicker, attaching themselves to Ruad like they were trying to hold him a little closer too.

"With light," I said softly, repeating Senan's words.

"Aye, with light," Ruad confirmed.

We sat there, tangled up in each other for a while, waiting for Declan and Senan. I knew I should move but I couldn't bear it just yet.

# CHAPTER 13

I woke up confused and sore. The bedroom wasn't familiar, and I sat up in a panic before remembering the main bedroom that was destroyed. All of last night came rushing back to me and I grabbed Declan to reassure myself.

"Hey, you're okay," he whispered in response to my obvious panic.

"I fell asleep," I said.

"You needed to after everything last night."

"But I didn't even know if you were okay. How could I fall asleep like that?"

"Hey, it's okay. When we came back, Ruad said you needed to calm down, and he wanted you to rest peacefully so he did a little spell. He carried you back here and tucked you in and it seems you rested just fine."

"Too fine. I feel like it's still last night. I don't remember it ending."

"It's over, babe. They're all gone," he said as he gathered me in his arms.

The comfort of his embrace was followed by the now familiar pang of guilt. I had kissed Ruad, and I had to tell him.

I must have cringed because Declan pulled me back to look at me.

"What is it, Bridget?"

"I kissed Ruad. And then he kissed me," I blurted out, ducking my head.

I tried to escape his embrace, but he pulled me closer. Refusing to meet his eyes, I just sat there awaiting my punishment.

He tried to get me to meet his eyes by lifting my chin as Ruad had done but I resisted. My cowardice wouldn't allow it.

"Hey, look at me," he said softly.

Reluctantly I glanced sideways at him. He chided me more until I looked fully at him.

"Bridget, I don't know how many more times I have to tell you that I know you would never betray me. Ruad explained the whole to me, and if anything it's him I'm mad at but I'll tell you, I can't blame the guy.

"If he loves you anything like I love you, then he's a glutton for punishment. I wouldn't be able to stand back and leave you be. And I won't. I know your intentions were true, Bridget. I hope you know mine are too."

"What's wrong with you?" I joked.

"Me? You're the one kissing other men!"

"I was trying to save his life!"

"I know! That's why I'm not mad. And then he kissed you. Which I'm not thrilled about, but tell me Bridget, are you leaving me for him?"

"No, you know I'm not."

"Okay, then it's alright Bridget, truly. You meant no harm to me, only well for him. I can't say I wish you'd let him die instead so what other choice do I have?"

"I don't know, you just never respond the way I anticipate you will," I said shaking my head.

"Because I respond with love and understanding, something you've been in short supply of. Which only makes me love you more."

"I don't know why," I whispered.

"You don't know why. You don't listen, Bridget. I said I love you, and you argue it. You can't tell me not to love and accept you the way you are, because I do."

"But why? I don't deserve it," I whispered.

There it was. The unspoken truth I couldn't get past. I wasn't worthy.

"You do," he said fervently. "Bridget, you're beautiful, strong, smart, sweet, funny, all of these wonderful things. Why would you not deserve love?"

I really didn't have an answer to that, so I shrugged slightly.

"Bridget, the people that hurt you did so not because you weren't worthy of love and kindness but because you were more than worthy and that threatens small people.

"Small people need to be more important at all times, and they do so by hurting other people. They hurt people because they are incapable of loving themselves and it's the only way they have power.

"And you responded with love and kindness because of your *goodness,* Bridget, don't you see that?

"But your goodness allowed them to keep hurting you because you chose to see the best in them. Can't you see that's why I love you? That you choose to love even when it hurts? That you see past the brokenness in other people to the small part in them that's good? Can't you see that's why I love you? I don't see brokenness when I see you, I see strength."

"It's called stupidity," I mumbled.

"It was not your finest hour," he said with a wink. "But I know for one why you tried so hard. The other one, not so much. I'll call that one circumstantial." He rolled his eyes slightly, joking.

He meant Nick there.

"You did the best you could, and you chose to love instead of let the world make you bitter. That's called courage, bravery, strength. Not stupidity.

"You tried to show love to people who weren't worthy of *you,* my love. Don't ever confuse their loss with yours. They didn't know how precious you are, and that's their loss and your gain.

"And you DID win, even if it doesn't always feel like it. You still care for them and wish them well when they would deserve it if you didn't. You took your pain, and you used it as fuel for good.

"You think I haven't overheard your conversations at work? That I don't know that customers come to see you over and over again because you listen to their troubles with kindness and understanding, without judgment?

"That, after all of the horrible things that have been done to you, it only steeled your reserve to do better. You used those horrible things to make yourself better, not bitter.

"I know how hard you push yourself to open your mind and your heart even wider after people abuse it. That you try to love them as they are not as you wish they were. And I know the toll it takes on you too, love.

"The world keeps giving you lemons and you keep making lemonade. And then you share that gift with the world so someone else in pain can have the support you never did. You make the difficult decision to open your heart again every time when no one would blame you if you closed it off for good.

"Ruad sees what I see in you. He knows your heart is true and pure, and *good*, Bridget. Lord knows how good you are.

"I think that's why I don't mind so much. You deserve more than you've been given to this point. Hell, you didn't deserve what you've gotten is more like it.

"And I'll be damned if I'm the one to keep you from anything that makes you happy. I can't be as selfless as Ruad, because I won't give you up even if you ask, but I won't force you to let him go either."

"I'm not that good though, Declan,"

"Aye, you've done some stupid things, I'll grant you, but not *bad* things Bridget. Not malicious things. Trying to drown your sorrows doesn't make you bad, it makes you down on your luck. It makes you human."

"You know it's more than that."

"And you know I've made similar mistakes as you. I've been known to bury my sorrows in bed with women as much as I've been known to drown them at the bottom of a bottle. I know what pain like that does to a person. Does it make you not love me?"

"You know it doesn't, jealous maybe," I said as I rolled my eyes.

What a hypocrite I was.

"Then why can't I love you flaws and all?"

"Because you shouldn't," I said with a laugh.

"Maybe you just want me to be jealous."

"It doesn't hurt."

"And you just argue for the sake of arguing," he said laughing too.

"I am Irish,"

"Stubborn lot we are," he said kissing me finally.

I didn't feel much more reassured, but I at least didn't feel like I was being torn in half either anymore. So that was an improvement.

It wasn't that I didn't appreciate Declan and his love for me, but trauma does weird things to people.

I appreciated his words in ways that words couldn't express. But he knew that, and if I wasn't sure the squeeze of his hand told me that he did.

The tightening in my chest eased a little. Maybe he really did love me. Rather, maybe he *could* love me, flaws and all.

I was always fighting the belief in my head that I wasn't worthy of love and Declan tackled it the best way he could. With patience. And a ton of understanding.

"Now quit your pity party. Let's get some coffee and breakfast," he said as he smacked my butt.

"It's not a pity party."

"Don't I know it, love."

Following him to the kitchen I was surprised to find Ruad at the table already, coffee made and breakfast ready. This wasn't so bad after all.

Hearing noises from the kitchen I realized it must be Loretta that made everything for us. Ruad raised an eyebrow at me, and I rolled mine.

Why did they both have the ability to read my mind so easily? After a lifetime of being misunderstood I wasn't sure if it was comforting or not to have people know me so intimately.

Sometimes I wanted to kick them out of my head. Other times it was nice not having to explain myself.

It was definitely nice not having to explain my intentions all the time. That much I did know.

"Good morning, did you sleep well?" Ruad asked.

I wasn't sure if he was teasing or genuine, but I did sleep well.

"Yes, your spell worked just fine. But I would appreciate it if you didn't do it again."

"You needed it. The adrenaline crash would have made you anxious and shaky. I knew Declan and Senan were fine. But I can warn you next time, deal?" he conceded.

"Deal," I said reluctantly.

"But what we didn't yet discuss was what exactly did happen last night," Ruad started.

"Coffee," I said.

They both laughed. I was useless without it.

Declan poured me a cup and Ruad made me a plate of food and they each placed it in front of me. I laughed at the oddity of our little love triangle, but I thanked them each in turn. If they could accept it, then I guess I could too.

I sat and ate my breakfast and drank coffee while I listened to them regale the accounts of last night. Ruad was right about the adrenaline affecting me and I ate three plates of food before they finished talking. I listened and chimed in as I ate, talking around a mouth full of food and not caring in the slightest. They loved me after all.

After I said my part we pieced it all together. Declan must have gotten the hex bag when we were in Senan's world. Failinis and Enbarr weren't with him, and we were all occupied. In his underwear was another story but any sprite could have done it.

Senan and I were attacked by Evil, and we defeated him. Nick was possessed or something like it. While we battled Evil Ruad had Carman to himself. She had placed a few runes that summoned him and kept him engaged in battle with her.

He reassured me he wasn't hurt, and indeed what cuts and bruises that were there last night were gone. Carman was powerful, but she was clever more than strong. The rune kept him engaged because he couldn't leave since he was summoned. Then she had used spells to directly negate his strengths.

He swears he would have won even with Darkness dragging him under. Ruad was a God, and she was a witch. No competition, he said.

The gleam in his eye led me to believe him. I would hate to have someone look at me with eyes like that. But nonetheless, I was glad we helped.

Declan had found Darkness's body as it was glowing from the magic I was putting into Ruad. They used Senan's magic to eliminate his physical body while I worked on his spirit form.

After Ruad woke up, I fell asleep. They came back and Senan helped Nick to wherever Nick needed to go. Far away from me was all I cared about. I was reassured there would be someone keeping an eye on him from now on. I assumed they meant Senan.

We all felt pretty safe in that this Carman business was finished. Ruad did caution that the Queen of Elphame was likely to continue to cause problems but not to worry just yet about it. If we didn't take time to relax and recover we'd be useless anyway.

I agreed.

As breakfast wound to a close, I started to feel anxious. I didn't particularly want to part with Ruad, and I think we all kind of knew it.

"Walk me out?" Ruad asked me.

Declan winked at me in encouragement, and I obliged.

At the door I didn't know what to say, so we hugged instead. Another one of those moments when I was grateful he knew my innermost thoughts. If I had spoken I would have cried.

"I'm never far," he said.

I knew what he meant. Knew he would be watching from a distance. It was the distance part I wasn't a fan of, but I knew I couldn't have my cake and eat it too.

Ruad kissed the top of my head and I placed one on his cheek. We gave a small smile and a squeeze of each other's hand, and he was gone in a blink, my hand still outstretched. Closing the door with a sigh, I turned to find Loretta standing there.

"Hi, Loretta. Thank you for breakfast, everything was lovely," I said to her.

"Oh, good, I'm glad you enjoyed your last meal," she said as she touched my shoulder.

I had a moment to register her odd statement before everything went black.

———————————

# ACKNOWLEDGEMENT

Thank you to my wonderful friends that helped design the cover of this book, Les, and edit this book, Susan. Without the two of you this book wouldn't exist!

Of course to my wonderful and supportive husband and family. Thanks for believing in me when I couldn't.

And to my kids, you were a hindrance to the writing process (haha) but my main inspiration and I love you more than you'll ever know!

# ABOUT THE AUTHOR

## Shea Hulse

Shea is a wife and mother of two. When she is not writing she enjoys traveling with her family. She helps women master their mindset and build successful online businesses of their own so they can live their best lives. She and her husband have been sober for over four years and she enjoys spreading positivity to others who may be struggling in life.

# BOOKS IN THIS SERIES

*A Celtic Romance Series*
Bridget and Declan face supernatural foes with the help of their new paranormal friends.

## Fireflies

In my frenzy, I ran into something without realizing it. Big hands closed over my shoulders as I gripped the chest they belonged to. Under other circumstances, I'd be elated. Green eyes stared back at me, his reddish hair hidden beneath a baseball cap, huge frame swallowing mine easily.

Bridget had never considered herself special, odd sure, but nothing worth looking at twice. And she had never cared to be looked at twice, either.

Until Declan, that is.

Then one night Bridget is approached by a strange (and large) dog. Rescued by Declan, he reveals that Bridget may be special after all. And the dog has been sent to protect her.

Does she have the strength to defeat a powerful witch and her three sons? Why is Declan involved in magic and mystery, anyway? And can she save Ruad, her handsome mentor in this new world? As they dig deeper, they uncover that they all have more in common than just their troubled pasts.

The Ulster Cycles are a part of Irish mythology, and this novel depicts characters from the old stories in a new and creative light. While much is taken from these oral stories, this novel is a historical romance loosely based on them.

With magic, mystery, and romance involved, this is a novel about discovering your hidden potential and celebrating your authentic self.

## Dragonflies

To be announced.

## Butterflies

To be announced.

Printed in Great Britain
by Amazon

21211265R00129